MERCENARY

LITTLE DEATH BRINGER

USA TODAY BESTSELLING AUTHOR
CATHERINE BANKS

Mercenary by Catherine Banks

This is a work of fiction. Names, characters, places and incidents either are the product of the author's imagination or are used fictitiously. Any resemblance to actual persons, living or dead, events, or locales is entirely coincidental.

Turbo Kitten Industries™

P.O. Box 5012, Galt, CA 95632
www.catherinebanks.com

TURBO KITTEN

To Lacey, Jackie, and the other fans who became my friends. Thank you for your continued support.

A special thanks to my best friend and husband, Avery, for his patience and understanding while I participated in NaNoWriMo to write this book.

"Keep your elbows down and off of the table, Marin," Amadis, Queen of the Elves and my foster mother, ordered me as I sat at one of the large mahogany tables inside the exquisite ballroom where the Elves held their balls each year. The balls were always extravagant and filled with ladies in beautiful dresses and men in tuxedos dancing, flirting and clinking glasses appropriately. It was all out of my league and yet I had to attend them every year, unless I was at school.

At sixteen years old, I was supposed to know how to be a proper lady already. Unfortunately for Mother, I was more skilled at the manly arts of hunting and killing than crafts and crumpets. She kept strong and continued to train me despite my boorish tendencies and I was finally learning a few things. I picked up the proper fork and took a small, ladylike bite of the salad and then chewed slowly with my lips closed.

"Well done!" she said happily, clapping her hands together to show how pleased she was. When she was happy, Mother glowed and would have put angels to shame if they existed. She was gorgeous with fair skin, silver hair and pointed ears. When I'd first come to live with the Elves, I had been envious of their pointed ears, silver hair, and beauty. At one point, I had felt poorly about myself for not being an Elf, but Mother assured me that there was nothing wrong with being a human and told me I was a beautiful human. I wasn't sure if I believed her or not, but I stopped being overly envious of the Elves and just accepted myself as I was. I didn't know if I was pretty or not, but it hadn't bothered me, until the past year.

"Alright, we are done for the day," she said. "Go ahead and go change."

I kissed her cheek and walked quickly out of the ballroom and to my room to change. It took me fifteen minutes just to get out of the dress with all of its tiny buttons, but once I was out of the dress and in my pants and sleeveless shirt, I finally felt like myself. Mother meant well and I did try to behave, but I preferred being outside, getting dirty, and fighting to being clean, inside the castle, and sipping tea.

I stared at my reflection in the mirror and inspected my thin frame with a little muscle in the right places and feminine curves in the right places as well. My long blonde and brown hair hung to my back and sighed. There were so many areas for improvement.

I dismissed the things I could not fix on myself and ran out the back door of the castle. Even if it were possible to change my physical appearance, I wouldn't have done it. I am who I am and I can only change certain things and I accepted that...or at least that's what I repeated in my head several times a day.

I continued on my way to the fighting arena that was built over one thousand years ago. The sand arena held many memories for me, but I knew it held even more for the Elves that lived there. Humans envied the Elven race because the Elves were one of the few races which were immortal. They could be killed, but they would never die of old age or illness and at their oldest only looked to be in their late thirties. For humans who valued beauty and youth since they only had them for a few years, they wished for a way to become an immortal.

The sand arena was over one hundred feet in diameter and had wooden boards around the outer edges. The male Elves that lived in the kingdom came every Saturday to train and spar with each other. Fighting prowess was highly regarded in the kingdom and those that were poor fighters weren't well thought of and generally didn't come to many functions.

As I walked up, I realized that a much larger group had come than usual and there were well over three hundred Elves around the arena. As soon as I was noticed, they all turned and smiled at me. Every Elf had pointed ears and ninety percent had silver hair, which made them fairly easy to spot out in the rest of the world. I walked through the crowd, receiving pats on the back from the older Elves and smiles from the younger ones until I came to the front to see who was fighting in the arena.

I stood on the bottom rail of the fence to look over

just as I had done every Saturday since I was five years old and folded my arms on top of the fence. Cesar had brought me out here after witnessing a few of my fights with other four and five-year-old male Elves and decided that I needed an outlet and some training since I seemed determined to continue on a path of fighting. Mother had been against it at first, but they told me that it truly did help my temper and I stopped fighting others except when in the arena or when my life or honor was on the line.

I watched as Cesar, King of the Elves and my foster father, fought hand to hand with Favian, Prince of the Elves and my best friend. Favian was fast and an incredibly better fighter than me, but he still had a lot to learn before he could best his father. I watched their fight and smiled as my two favorite males battled each other. A few minutes later Favian was pinned to the ground by Father who had a wide smile on his face. "Still too slow, Son," Father said.

I clapped my hands and whistled. "Good job! Nice fake pinning, Favian."

Father looked at me curiously a moment and that was all it took for Favian to escape the pin and whip around his father to put him in a choke hold. "Never take your eye off of your opponent, Father."

The crowd cheered and laughed and Father patted his son's arm. "I concede. You won, but only because of Marin's trickery."

I pretended to look offended. "Me use trickery? I would never do such a thing."

"Come into the ring and let us see how much you've learned," Kato, Father's guard and a man who had spent much of my childhood playing with me and carving toys from wood for me, said. He was like an uncle to me and I never took his love for me for granted.

I jumped into the ring and walked as though I were holding up a dress in my fingertips. "Sir, I am but a sweet maiden who is appalled at your crude ways and cruel words."

Kato tossed a sword to me and I caught it easily. "You, my dearest child, are a very adept liar. It frightens me quite a bit."

I spun the sword and said, "I learned from the best," and bowed to him. The crowd laughed at our banter and I smiled happily.

He smiled back at me and then took a ready stance. "Come at me, girl. Let us see if you can last more than three seconds today." I took a ready stance and then charged forward, slashing downwards and then sideways, but of course he easily dodged both attacks and attacked me, forcing me on the defensive. I rolled to the right to avoid his strikes and then kicked at his legs, but my timing was poor because he chose that moment to strike downwards. I rolled to the right just in time to avoid the blow, but that was also because he drew back enough to stop the blade and not cut me.

I stood up and sighed. "How long was that?"

"Four seconds," Father said from the fence.

I groaned and Kato patted my back. "That's better than last time," he consoled me.

"Only because you pulled back that last strike," I grumbled angrily.

"Come, you and I need to fight," Jovan said. Jovan

was one of the younger males who I often sparred with and one of the many who came to spar with Favian. He was also one of the few Elves, whom I found to be unattractive. He had similar features, but there was something off with his symmetry that made him ugly to me. He was nice and I had no problems with him, so he and I had developed a sort of warrior friendship.

I bowed to Kato and then turned to face Jovan. "Swords or hands?" I asked.

"Swords because obviously you need much more practice."

I stuck my tongue out at him and then walked to the center of the ring and took a ready stance. "I take it you aren't going to go easy on me, are you?" I guessed.

He smiled evilly. "Do I ever?" I smiled at him in response.

He lunged forward and I was forced to act and react instead of plan moves. He did hold back, despite his claim. Otherwise, I would have been dead within seconds, but he did so in a way that kept me fighting and helped me learn.

We sparred for at least ten minutes and then I didn't see his fake and I had his sword against my throat. "Dang," I said sadly.

He smiled and removed his sword. "You are learning and you are doing a lot better than last year."

"Yes, but I am still only at a toddler Elf's level," I complained as we walked out of the arena to let others spar.

He patted my back. "You cannot compare yourself to us, you know this."

"It's just that I feel that I can do better, but I can't

seem to figure out how to unlock it."

"It just takes practice and time. You don't think Kato learned to be as good as he is in sixteen years, do you?"

I laughed. "I know they have many years on me, but that's another problem. My race only lives to be eighty years old at the most! I'll never be able to have as much training as you guys do. I'll only have forty years of real training available and then after that I'll be degrading into an old woman."

"I thought we had agreed not to discuss things like this," Favian said as he walked up to me with his shirt off, mopping up the sweat on his upper body with it.

Favian had the telltale elf characteristics of silver hair and pointed ears, but even after meeting every Elf in the Kingdom, I could easily say that he was the most handsome Elf I had ever seen. Drool built up within my mouth and I was forced to turn away from him. Why did I react to him in such a way? I hadn't felt these sensations two or three years ago and now all of a sudden, I found myself thinking ludicrous things such as kissing him.

"She only speaks the truth," Jovan said.

"We do not speak of it," Favian said angrily.

"Right," I said. "We must not speak of my impending doom. One which will end while Favian is still technically a child to the Elves," I said bitterly before walking away. I didn't usually get upset about it because I knew it was going to happen, but today it bothered me. It really bothered me that I was going to look old and haggard while Favian looked exactly as he did now. I would die while he was in his youth.

It was an awful feeling and one I did not talk about because it hurt too much.

I headed passed the arena and continued through the fields until I made it to the river. The Elves had a way with nature that ensured the Kingdom was always beautiful with blooming flowers and clear flowing rivers. I sat down on the edge of a high rocky area and looked down at the fast-moving water. Fish swam with the current in the waters in a variety of colors that made the whole area even more beautiful.

I had wished on every star to be granted some miracle which would give me the type of longevity the Elves experienced, but alas wishing on stars did not work. I had prayed to the God and Goddess and that had failed as well. I had had to come to the realization when I was only six years old, that I would never live as long as Favian. The only reassuring part was that I wouldn't have to bear witness to his death.

"Marin," Favian whispered as he sat down next to me. "I thought we were over this?"

"I will never be *over* it, Favian. I am going to die before you and I am going to get old and look disgusting while you look as you do currently. It is always in the back of my mind."

"You know I will not care what you look like. You are my best friend and you shall always be so."

The only problem was that I cared. "Yes, you shall be King and be friends with an old, grouchy human woman."

"The only difference from now will be your age," he teased me. I ignored the tease and tossed a pebble into the water. "What is really bothering you?" he asked. "You have been acting differently since your birthday."

I turned and looked at his perfectly proportioned body and the perfectly pointed ears and sighed. "It's nothing. Just realizing that my death is approaching ever closer each year." It was a lie, but I couldn't tell him that the real reason I was upset was because my reactions and feelings towards him had changed this past year and I didn't know why or what it meant.

"You will live a long and happy life," he assured me.

"I would be happy if I could live longer than a human," I whispered.

"If there were a way to change that for you, I would. You know that, right?"

I hugged him and then leaned my head against his shoulder. "You really are my best friend. The only solace I have is that I will never have to see you die."

He pushed me away and stared into my eyes. "Do not talk of such things."

"It's the truth," I whispered.

"You think I like to remember that I will have to watch you die? Do you think I enjoy knowing that I will have to watch you get old and feeble and bear witness to your death?! It is a burden that I must bear and I hate it."

I knew he wasn't trying to be mean and yet his words stung. I stood up and turned away from him. "Then perhaps we would be better off not being friends. Then neither of us would have to endure this."

"You are overreacting yet again," he said angrily.

I wasn't trying to be childish. It truly made sense. "Or perhaps I am making better sense than ever before. You are going to be King. You are going to begin courting female Elves within the next year. I am only impeding that process by dragging you off on adventures. Maybe I should leave," I said as I started walking away.

"You are being childish and foolish," he called to me as he started following. "Stop this nonsense and let's go for a ride."

"It is not foolishness or childishness. It is the first smart thing I have ever done. From now on you should spend more time with your Elven friends and not me. I will ride with you to the Academy and once my training is complete, I will move out of the Elven Kingdom and remove this burden from your shoulders."

"I did not mean it like that and you know it!" he yelled as he caught up to me.

I turned to him and met his eyes with a slight smile. "I know you didn't, but it is the truth. You are my best friend and I must do what is best for you. I will see you Monday when we leave for the Academy."

"Pushing me away won't fix this. You will only cause yourself and me more pain. Do not do this," he whispered.

"Favian!" Jovan called. "The King wants you at the arena."

"Marin," Favian whispered. "Come with me."

I straightened my back and continued on my way to the castle. It pained me to think of life without Favian, but I wanted what is best for him. I reached to open the door and Favian opened it for me. "What are you doing?" I asked him in shock.

"If you won't come with me, then I will come with you."

"Favian, Father summoned you."

"Yes, but you are my partner and wherever you go, I go."

"I am trying to save us both," I whispered.

"You are being a stubborn, rash girl and until you realize that it would be far worse for us to stop being friends than deal with the issues in seventy years, I will ignore your words and stay by your side."

"You really aren't going to let me do this, are you?" I asked with a sigh.

He smiled. "I am your best friend and I will always be your best friend. Even if you try to do stupid things that you think are in my best interest."

"You are so stubborn."

"You are very rash," he whispered as he stepped forward and hugged me.

"I don't want to be a burden on you," I whispered from within his arms.

"You have never been a burden. You have always just been my friend."

"You make being angry at you very difficult," I said with a laugh.

"It's part of my charm as Prince. If even my best friend cannot stay mad at me, then the entire kingdom has no hope."

I pulled out of his embrace and said, "I'm sorry." I hated it when my girly emotions got the better of me.

He punched my shoulder softly. "No worries. I know that sometimes you have to have some drama or your girl brain will explode."

"I was not being dramatic!" I said angrily. "Oh, but you were."

"Weren't you summoned to go somewhere?" I asked him with a scowl.

He grabbed my hand and dragged me away from the castle and back towards the arena. "Yes, we were."

As much as I hated to admit it, I would have been miserable had he allowed me to go through with my plan. I couldn't imagine life without Favian. He was with me all of the time and I planned all of my moves according to his presence. I had really been trying to help us, but I was glad I couldn't go through with it.

We arrived at the arena to find Kato and Father sparring. I watched the two best friends with awe as I leaned against the fence. They moved almost too fast for me to keep track of. Their match went on and on and seemed as if it would never end, but then Kato stepped back and dropped his sword. "I submit. I will die of dehydration if I do not stop this match."

Father sighed. "You are such a wimp about the sun. How did I ever end up with you as a guard?"

Kato picked his sword back up and sheathed it. "You picked me, remember?"

Father smiled. "Yes, one of my few mistakes."

Kato laughed and then Father laughed with him. Theirs was a five-hundred-year-old friendship, something I could only dream of. I turned to Favian and he put his arm around my shoulders and squeezed. "See, friends have spats, but you must always stay together. I bet if you asked Father he could tell you of many times where he and Kato argued or didn't see eye to eye."

"Alright, you made your point. I will not try to separate us again."

He released me and hopped over the fence. "You called for me, Father?"

Father nodded. "Yes. I'd like you to take Jovan and some of the others out to check on the Pegasus herd. They haven't come up here in a week, which is not like them."

My cheeriness plummeted and I began to walk away from the arena. Only Elves were allowed to venture out into the Pegasus' area of the Kingdom. They were a race of flying horses created by Father and he had made the rule when he created them that only Elves could go to their fields. I would be forced to stay at the castle and be bored.

Kato walked beside me and said, "Do not look so sullen. He made that rule one hundred years before they adopted you."

"I know, Kato, but it still sucks."

"You have met the Pegasus before, right?" I nodded. "And you've ridden one?" I nodded again. "So then why are you upset? It's one of only two things you are not allowed to do here. You should be happy. You are the only human in existence to have ridden a Pegasus."

I groaned. "Alright, Kato I get it. I'm being silly, but I do wish I could go, especially if there is going to be trouble."

"Prince Favian can handle whatever it is," Kato

assured me. I rolled my eyes. "Duh."

Kato laughed and put his arm around me. "How about you and I go raid the kitchen and steal a piece of berry cake?"

"You raid the kitchen?" I asked in shock. "You never do anything bad."

He laughed. "I am known as the berry cake bandit. Now, if you promise to be good, I will show you the best way to sneak into the kitchen and the best escape route."

Somehow, he always knew what to say or do to ease my distress and make me smile. I followed him around to the side of the castle and then let him lead me through a secret opening even I had not found yet. Ten minutes later we had snuck into the kitchen, grabbed a piece of cake and were almost out completely free, when the chef came in and spotted us.

"Cake thieves!" He yelled. "Kato, I will get you for this!"

"Run!" Kato said and then booked it to the left, out another door I had never noticed. It led into the ballroom, which would have been great if Mother hadn't been sitting there waiting for me to begin our next lessons.

"Kato!" She said in a chastising tone. "I told you that when you steal cake, you must steal an extra piece for me."

Kato pulled a hidden piece out and set it on the table in front of her. "I always do as my Queen asks."

Mother clapped her hands together with a bright smile on her face like a child receiving a present and then took a bite from the cake. "Thank you!"

I stared at the two adult Elves, each over five hundred years old, stealing cake like adolescents and could not believe I had witnessed it. Favian would never believe me.

"Sit, let's eat our cake," Mother said as she took another bite.

Kato and I took seats at the table and we ate our cake and they shared stories of other cake heists over the years. I laughed until I cried. They were starting to share stories about my first discretions when I was only four years old and had just arrived at the Kingdom when Father walked in and eyed the crumbs on the table accusingly. "What is going on here?"

"We were just discussing Marin's first attempts to steal candy from the kitchen when she was only four years old and had first come here," Mother said with a smile. Kato tried to discreetly wipe the crumbs off of the table without Father noticing. Apparently, Father was not part of the cake heists.

Father sat down and laughed. "Yes, those were very entertaining, except when the chef caught you the one time and spanked you. You, being the girl that you are, refused to cry when he spanked you because you were too happy that you had managed to get a piece of candy and had eaten it before he had caught you."

I laughed and shook my head. "I hadn't realized I was so naughty when I was younger."

"Oh yes, your naughtiness started as soon as you arrived," Mother teased.

"Hello," Favian said as he entered. "What's going on?"

"Just reminiscing," Father said. "How fare the Pegasus?"

"They are fine, just being lazy in these Fall months," Favian said as he sat down beside me at the table.

"I think I'm going to head to bed," I said as I stood up. "Tomorrow is my last day to enjoy the delights of home and I want to be up early to enjoy them."

"I think I shall do the same. That sparring match with Father has tired me out," Favian said as he yawned. "Good night, Mother. Good night, Father. Kato."

"Good night children," Mother said.

"Good night everyone," I said with a wave as I followed Favian out of the ballroom where we had been.

"So why are you really heading out so early?" Favian asked accusingly as soon as the ballroom doors closed behind us.

"I really am exhausted," I told him. "I've been awake since before the sun rose this morning."

"So, you aren't going to sneak off somewhere?" he asked unbelievingly.

"No," I said seriously. "I really am going to bed."

Shock and disbelief were written on his face, but he knew I wouldn't lie to him about my plans for sneaking off. "Well in that case, I will see you tomorrow morning bright and early. Want to go for a ride through the fields tomorrow?"

I shook my head. "No, we will be doing a lot of riding the next day."

"I meant on a Pegasus," he said with a smirk. "Really?!" I asked excitedly.

He nodded. "One of them is coming to the castle tomorrow and he agreed to take you and me for a ride."

I beamed happily and hugged him. "Thank you. Thank you. Thank you!"

He laughed and patted my back. "Now get to bed."

I did as he said and went to bed and despite my excitement, I fell asleep dreaming of flying on a Pegasus across the fields of the Elven Kingdom.

I knew it was late and getting later by the second, especially since I still had to get changed, but I couldn't say anything to Mother since it would only upset her. She was my foster mother after all and I strived to please her and do my best since I wasn't her born daughter and they had given me so much over the years. Despite my knowledge of how late it was, I sat at one of the many tables in the ballroom preparing tea in a tea pot and then pouring it into cups like a lady would when serving guests.

Personally, I believed people could serve themselves just as well as I could, but I did as Mother asked and practiced serving.

"Marin!" Favian yelled as he rushed into the ballroom.

I set the teapot down, stood slowly and adjusted the dress appropriately as I moved away from the table. I was still in Mother's training and had to follow her rules even though all I wanted to do was run to

Favian and then out of the room. I curtsied to Favian and asked, "How may I assist you, Prince Favian?"

He glanced at Mother who was giving him the evil stare and sighed in exasperation. He had been trained since he was born to be a proper Prince, so this was nothing new to him. He just hated practicing when it wasn't necessary. He bowed to me and then picked my hand up and kissed the back of it softly. The kiss sent tingles up my arm to my spine, but I kept perfectly still so that he wouldn't notice. "It is a pleasure to see you, Lady Marin. I have come seeking your company as it is time to leave the Elven Kingdom and travel. We are *late*. It is the afternoon of Sunday and we shall not make it on time to the Academy as it is."

"That is not a proper way to speak to a lady," Mother said with a weary sigh. "Alright, be on your way children."

I picked the sides of the dress up to keep from tripping on it and ran to her, kissing her cheek, before darting out of the ballroom and down the hallway. Favian was on my heels as we ran and followed me up the staircase made of exquisitely carved white elm and into my room, which was the first door on the left at the top of the stairs. "Why must you always be in these inconveniently difficult to remove dresses when it's time to go?" he complained as I kicked off my heels.

My room oozed with femininity from the pink lace curtains to the frilly and fluffy down comforter, which despite its ugliness was incredibly warm. I had tried to incorporate my own tastes into the room, but every time I left for the Academy, Mother raided my room and removed anything masculine.

"Just start unbuttoning the dress quickly or we will be even later to school," I said as I pulled off the white satin gloves and began removing the various jewelry items she forced me to wear and put them away inside the jewelry box on the vanity. They were all items I didn't have interest in, but valued since they were gifts from Mother and I knew she enjoyed seeing me wear them. I kept them in the jewelry box which Kato had carved for me.

Favian worked expertly, unbuttoning the fifty little buttons extremely quickly. I bit my tongue to keep from asking how he had gained such experience in unbuttoning the dress so quickly. "Now hurry and change. I'll go get the horses ready," he said irritably.

I nodded in understanding and stepped out of the dress, tossing it onto the large fluffy and incredibly comfortable bed and then grabbed my pants and long-sleeved shirt that were mandatory wear at school. It was my sixth and last year at the school and I was determined to be the first girl to have ever attended or finished the Academy.

Favian and I both attended Macon Academy, a school for those gifted in fighting. The school was created to teach boys to become men and to train them to be able to get jobs as Mercenaries, guards, or to become part of the human King's Army. My goal was to become a Protector, which was the highest level a Mercenary could achieve. Protectors went around the countryside aiding towns, villages or people who needed it, or on missions from the various Kings of the world. It was a highly respected job and I craved to become one more than anything in the world. It was my life's goal.

I was the first girl allowed to join the school and I worked hard every day to prove that I had just as much right to be there as the males of the various species that also attended the school.

After tying my leather boots on, I grabbed my bag of clothes from the floor and double checked that I had everything necessary for the trip to school and the last three months of school.

"Ready?" Father asked from behind me.

I turned with a smile for the King of the Elves and bowed. "I am."

He was tall and thin, but looks were very deceiving when it came to Elves. Though he looked weak, I'd seen Father pick a fifty-foot tree up and throw it over two hundred yards. Their weak appearance and hidden strength was one of the defenses which had kept the Elves and their land safe the past one thousand years. He had fair skin like Mother, but was one of the few Elves with black hair. He had found me on the side of the road when I was four years old and taken me in, raising me as if I were his own child. I had never felt like a step child or felt like I was a burden to them, which had made growing up much easier than it might have been if another human had found me.

I secured my belt which held my sword and sheath and two throwing knives, tied my cloak on, and then picked up my bag.

He held out his hand for my bag and I obediently gave it to him. One did not disobey the king. "Kato and I will be at your graduation ceremony in three months. Train hard and beat the hell out of the boys."

I smiled at him. "I shall try my hardest."

"I expect nothing less," he said in his fake serious tone. He gave me the same speeches he gave Favian, but we both knew that he wouldn't have cared if I dropped out of the school and decided to stay and be a lady at the castle. He would have simply kissed my cheek and told me to do what I loved and that made me love him even more than I would have to begin with.

We walked from my room, down the winding staircase and down the hallways which were lined with various murals of the previous rulers of the kingdom. I stopped next to the last mural and smiled at the small painting of a little human girl directly below the mural of Mother, Father, and Favian. I'd painted it when I was ten years old, wanting to be part of the family mural since I was adopted into the family. Father had ordered the painting to be kept, which had made me happier than the pony he'd bought me that year for my birthday.

"Marin?" he asked softly. "Are you alright?"

I turned and smiled at him. "Yes, just recalling the time I painted this."

He smiled back at me. "Lorimer was very upset that you'd done it."

Lorimer was the one in charge of keeping the castle in pristine condition. I had been a thorn in his side since I had arrived. "He had chased me around the castle with a willow branch, trying to corner me so that he could spank me. Even for an old Elf, he was quick on his feet. He almost got me and then you stopped him."

"Yes, I remember that day very well," he said with a smile. "Come, we must get you off to school."

I followed him as we walked into the main entryway and then out through the main doors, which were solid gold and incredibly heavy. Of course, when Father pushed them open, they appeared to weigh no more than a leaf. Favian stood in the courtyard holding our two horses, Fire and Ice. Fire and Ice were twins born to Mother's mare and of Father's stallion, the greatest horses in all of the lands. Fire had a red or sorrel coat while Ice had a bluish-white coat, which were the indicators of their names. We had been only ten years old when the horses had been born and they were the best names that we could come up with at the time. The horses dozed in boredom beside Favian as he talked to Amile, a pretty female Elf only one year my junior. A strange anger filled me and the idea of throwing a rock at Amile's head seemed like a stunningly good idea. I shook my head to clear the ridiculousness and walked to Fire who swiveled her ears in my direction when she noticed me.

These new feelings had started coming over me only this past year whenever I saw females with Favian. I didn't understand it and I didn't like it, not one bit.

Father tied my bag to Fire's saddle and then hugged me tightly. "Be safe, Daughter."

I hugged him back and then kissed his cheek. "Rule kindly, Father."

It was the same goodbye we'd said a hundred times as I'd left from vacation to return to school, yet today it felt different for some reason. I mounted

Fire and pet her neck. "Hello beautiful mare. Are you ready for a run?"

Fire nickered and pranced to show me her enthusiasm.

I looked over at Amile and Favian, still talking next to Ice and noticed the new necklace on Favian's neck. I had given him a twine and shell necklace two years ago on his birthday that had taken me six days to make. Most girls could have made the necklace in one day, but my lack of womanly skills had made the task almost impossible. He had told me he truly liked it and hadn't taken it off since then, but apparently, he had found a necklace he liked better now.

"Farewell, Prince Favian," Amile said with a flirtatious smile.

My anger skyrocketed and I nudged Fire, making her turn her rump into Amile's side, which made Amile stumble. "My apologies!" I yelled as I turned Fire and tightened the reins, acting as though I were correcting her. "She is full of energy today."

Amile smoothed down her dress and smiled at me. "She seems to take after her owner in so many regards."

"Let's go," Favian said seriously, giving me his angry stare and telling me silently to leave Amile alone.

I waved to Father and Kato who had come outside to see us off and then squeezed my legs around Fire's sides. She launched forward and cantered quickly to the front gate which was being held open by the guards. I waved to them as I went through the gates and then we passed through the magical barrier that surrounded the kingdom to protect it from unwanted guests. The barrier felt like a blanket pressed around you that you had to break through when entering, but when exiting it simply felt like a warm breeze.

The Elven Kingdom was surrounded by forests, which had every type of animal known to this part of the world. Since the Elves were herbivores, the animals didn't need to fear coming near them and we were always blessed with a few rare animals in their habitats, eating, playing and existing. It was refreshing, since the last mission Favian and I had gone on had sent us to an area overpopulated by humans who ate meat and ended up almost killing off the entire animal population in their area. I ate meat as well, but I knew there were ways to control the animal populations without killing them off.

The trees around us were tall and glorious, some as old as the Elven Kingdom itself. I loved running through the forest and listening to the sound of the wind blowing through the leaves. Some of the Elves believed that the plants could speak to you and would come talk to the trees. I had never heard the plants or trees talk, but I did enjoy being around them.

I let Fire run for a few miles and then pulled her back to conserve her energy. Favian caught up to me, having started out slowly and asked, "Are you in a foul mood today?"

I wanted to snap at him, but I held in my anger since he had done nothing wrong. "You're wearing a new necklace," I noted quietly.

He looked down at the new necklace and frowned a moment. "It was a gift."

"From Amile," I finished.

He looked at me and shrugged. "Yes. Does it bother you that I accepted her gift?"

"Of course not," I said quickly. "I just..." I trailed off, not wanting to tell him the real reason I was upset. I couldn't explain that I was upset that he'd taken off the necklace I'd given him to wear hers. Did he like her more than me?

A deer and her fawn stood in the center of the road and our horses moved around them so as not to startle the fawn and make it run off and possibly injure itself. The doe watched us with calm eyes and held her ground as we passed by.

"Marin," he said kindly, drawing my attention back to him. "I am sorry if I've upset you somehow. We're partners, right?" I nodded. "And in order for our partnership to work you must tell me what I've done to upset you."

"It's nothing. Forget I mentioned it," I said as I tied and untied a knot in my reins to avoid looking at him.

Favian trotted up closer to me until our knees were rubbing as the horses walked and stared into my eyes. "Tell me."

He had beautiful grey eyes that swirled like fog when he was mad and glittered like gemstones when happy. He'd been my best friend since I was four and my partner in crime since I was six. Together we'd completed every task the Academy had thrown at us and together we'd fought over a hundred enemies. We were partners and worked as one flawless unit, but recently things had been changing and I did not like it.

"I do not care that you receive gifts from females.

I do not care that you flirt with them. I do not care because you and I are partners in battle, not physically. I do care when you remove gifts I have given you and replaced them with a gift from a different female, though. It's dumb and that's why I tried to get you to drop it, but I am female after all and I have stupid emotions I cannot control sometimes. Now that I've told you why I was upset at first, please forget I said it and let us return to normal," I said quickly, stumbling over some of my words just to get it all out and be done with it.

"Is that what you truly want? You want me to leave this necklace on instead of taking it off and throwing it away like I had planned to do?" he asked me.

I looked at him in shock. "What?"

He smiled. "You think I like this ugly necklace that that girl made? The only reason I took it was because that is what a polite Prince is expected to do. Mother would have been furious if she had heard that I refused a gift from a female. I was going to simply accept it and throw it away later, but then she insisted I put it on."

"You could have told her you didn't want to take the necklace off since it was a gift," I muttered.

"Then she would have been insulted because she knows it was a gift from you and it would have been a big ordeal. It was simpler to give in until we were gone."

Despite its ridiculousness I felt much better and happier now that he had explained it all to me.

"So, do you still want me to forget it or can I throw this ugly thing away and put the one I like back on?"

he asked me with a teasing smile.

"Don't be rude," I told him. "It is unbecoming of a Prince." I turned my face and hid the blush that was creeping into my cheeks.

He laughed. "Now you sound like Mother. I think you spent too much time with her this past month."

"I spent all my time with her," I said irritably. "She insisted that I had to finish learning the womanly skills necessary for when I became a lady at eighteen."

"Have you figured out how to hide your sword under your dress yet?" he asked me.

I laughed and turned back to face him. "No. I think I might have to settle for several daggers and needles instead."

It was our ongoing joke that I figure out ways to be able to combine my skills with the manly arts with that of my womanly arts, such as keeping a sword inside my dress. I'd had very little success so far because somehow Amadis always knew when I had things hidden on me that I wasn't supposed to have. It was like some weird sixth sense.

Fire's ears shot forward just as Favian drew his sword from its sheath and slowed Ice. "Riders, six of them, are moving fast this way."

Another Elf perk I envied, extremely good hearing. I kept my sword sheathed to appear as a delicate female human being escorted by an Elf. It was surprising how well that tactic worked on dumb men. The riders appeared on the horizon line, still barely visible to me, but in perfect sight for Favian. "Human bandits. Be ready."

I nodded at him and then draped my right leg over

my horn so that I was essentially riding side saddle instead of regular. Even though I was wearing pants, that wouldn't deter most men since putting women in pants was a common tactic to make them appear less helpless, which helped us make me look more helpless in the current situation.

The bandits spotted us finally and charged the horses forward to encircle us. They were all very hairy with facial hair so thick that I couldn't see any of their mouths. They all wore dirty leather outfits that needed a soaking and then a washing. I was sure they wouldn't smell very good either, but I didn't try to find out, beginning to breathe through my nose as they moved closer.

The leader moved his horse closer to me and I pulled on Fire's reins to move her closer to Ice and Favian, tucking my head down and widening my eyes as though I were scared of him. Luckily my cloak hid my sword so he couldn't see it on my belt to realize I wasn't scared of him or his hairiness.

"Don't be frightened pretty lady. We won't hurt you," he said as he circled us. I thought he might be smiling, but it was hard to tell if his mustache had moved upwards or not.

"Leave us be," Favian said. "Or I shall be forced to defend myself and the lady."

"One Elf isn't enough to take on six men," the leader said. "Especially not a young Elf such as you."

That was where they were wrong. I knew Favian's true strength and it frightened me sometimes. Never get on an Elf's bad side or you won't live to regret it.

"Last warning," Favian said and then smiled.

"We're going to wipe that smile right off your face," another of the bandits said angrily. Was that a frown or was his beard just particularly droopy?

The leader reached out towards me to try to grab me from my saddle and as soon as his arm was within reach, I grabbed it and jerked him towards me, pulling him from his saddle. I shrieked as though shocked and scared at what had happened and then the fight began. Favian killed two men instantly with his throwing knives in their throats before they could even draw their swords and then he moved towards the other three.

The leader pulled his sword just as I pulled mine and then he came at me. He must have realized I wasn't completely defenseless or he wouldn't be attacking me. I parried his blow and then stabbed him with one of my knives. "Not all of us are damsels in distress," I whispered before yanking my knife out.

He raised his sword to strike me and I plunged mine into his belly. He gargled in pain and then fell to the ground dead. I was right, they did stink. I turned just in time to duck a punch by one of the other bandits and caught a whiff of his stench which made me gag a moment before swinging at his face with my fist. Favian finished with the bandit he was fighting and turned to me. "Need help?" he asked.

I punched the bandit in his face and then blocked his return punch. "No, I'm fine," I said as I hit him in the throat with my hand. He stumbled backwards gasping for air and then pulled a knife from his belt. I moved to pull mine, but Favian had already thrown one of his into the man's throat, ending his life. I turned and frowned at him. "I was fine."

He ignored me, hopping off of Ice's back to retrieve his knives. "You were moving too slow. He could have stabbed you before you got your knife out."

"If you don't let me protect myself, I won't learn," I told him as I wiped my knife and sword on the bottom of my cloak to clean the blood off.

"You can learn at school with dull blades that won't kill you," he retorted. He was upset, but I had no idea why. I hadn't done anything wrong, well at least not that I could think of. "Quickly check them over," he ordered.

I searched each of the men, coming up with a measly forty coins. I was searching the leader, sure that I would find nothing, when I came across a small painted picture in his pocket. I stared at the picture in shock and couldn't move. It was me. Why would he have a picture of me?

"You find anything?" Favian asked.

I turned the picture over and found two lines of writing:

Kidnap alive. Bring to me.

No signature. No name. Favian took the picture from my hand, scaring me and making me jerk a knife from my belt in reaction. He looked at me in shock a moment until he read the writing and turned the picture over. "We're going back to see Father," he said angrily.

"No!" I yelled. "We are already late for school as it is. We cannot be any later."

"Someone sent these men after you, Marin. Don't you understand that?" he asked as he faced me.

"Yes, but they failed and we are only a day away from school. Whoever hired them won't have time to learn of their failure and hire new men before we arrive. And you know as well as I do that the Academy is impossible to break into."

I could see the decisions warring within him and crossed my fingers behind my back. This was a tough decision for him since he was the one who had vowed to protect me when I'd been found and brought to the castle. Now as my self-proclaimed protector, he had to decide which the best protection was, the Academy or the Elves where I would try to sneak away to return to school.

"I have to finish at the Academy," I pleaded with him. "I only have three months left. Please Favian. Please!"

He sighed. "Fine, but I'm sending word to Father about this." I smiled happily and hugged him. "Thank you."

He pushed me away and put the picture in his pocket. "Get on your horse."

I did as he asked and we rode off at a brisk pace towards the Academy. We would have to camp off the road later that night since we had gotten such a late start to the day and then we would reach the school by midday tomorrow. Macon would be very upset that we were half a day late, but the worst he would do was force us take an extra shift of guard duty.

I glanced at Favian to find him releasing his long

silver hair from the silver clip he wore to hold it back from covering his ears. He wasn't ashamed of his Elven heritage, but he found it beneficial to hide it sometimes. Other times it meant he was mad at me and hiding his ears because he knew I preferred his hair up and his ears out. I was pretty sure it was both things prompting him to let his hair down currently.

I wanted to talk with him or joke to lighten the mood, but he had his serious face on and that meant that for the next eight hours we were going to be riding in silence. Silence would have been fine if I wasn't slightly freaked out by the fact that someone had hired bandits to kidnap me. Why? Who on earth would want to kidnap me? And to what purpose? Were they going to use me for ransom from the Elves? That would only end up bad for the kidnappers. The Elves would agree to their terms and then as soon as I was safe again, they would send out assassins to kill those that had kidnapped me.

Had I angered someone so much that they wanted me dead? No, otherwise the note would not have said to kidnap me alive. Had I angered someone who would want to kidnap me? I wasn't the most loved person, but I didn't really have any true enemies, just some childish dislikes. Even the three jobs I had done had all ended well and hadn't created any enemies for me.

It seemed like minutes had passed when I realized that the sun was setting. "We'll set up camp now," Favian said as he steered Ice off of the road and we made our way through the trees to find a suitable camping spot. Luckily there wasn't much brush so the horses were able to walk easily into the forest. We stopped about a mile from the road at a spot just wide enough for our horses and us to sleep. I dismounted and grabbed the small water skin off of Favian's pack to fill with water. "What are you doing?" he asked.

I looked at the water skin and then at him. "Getting water obviously. I can hear a stream nearby."

"You can't go off alone," he said adamantly.

I glared at him. "I can protect myself, Favian. I have been going off in the forest alone since I was six."

"Someone tried to kidnap you, Marin. It's not safe for you to wander off alone."

I thrust the water skin at him angrily. "Then you go get water while I unsaddle the horses." He clenched his jaw, but walked in the direction of the stream. Elves could be so stubborn sometimes that it was infuriating. I removed Fire's bridle and saddle and she shook all over, shaking dust from her coat. Ice nudged my shoulder, impatient to be unsaddled as well. "Easy boy. I'm working on it." I set Fire's stuff on one side of the clearing and then unbridled and unsaddled Ice and set his stuff on the other side. "You two be nice and don't wander too far. And Fire, don't bite your brother anymore. Favian gets upset at me when he finds the teeth marks on Ice's coat."

Fire bobbed her head and then she and Ice trotted off into the forest in search of drink and food for themselves. The horses couldn't truly understand me, but they were trained extremely well and understood us better than most horses did. Elves were animal gurus and could train them to do just about anything. Favian and I had raised them since they were born and

35

trained them together. Irritably Ice was better trained than Fire, but I still loved her. The main thing they were trained to do in these situations was not to wander too far and to come galloping at our call. I made sure the clearing was empty of rocks and then shook out my bedroll and laid on it a moment to ensure it was comfortable. I opened the food pack on Favian's saddle to see what the chef had given us, keeping my fingers crossed for something good. Sadly, there was no meat since the Elves were herbivores so I was stuck with bread and leaves from plants which were supposed to be highly nutritious. I dug deeper and was excited to find a piece of berry cake, but left it in the bag, not wanting to eat it if it was for Favian only.

I sat on top of my bedroll chewing on the bread when Favian made it back. "Still in one piece," I told him sarcastically. He didn't look like he thought it was funny and simply tossed me the water skin. I took a swig from it and then tossed him back the half of the bread I didn't eat. Elven food was fortified with special ingredients which made it very filling and healthy so you could survive a long time on a little bit of food. "Good night," I said as I climbed into my bedroll.

"I accidentally dropped the necklace in the river," he said around his mouthfuls. "It was swept away too fast for me to grab."

"Tragic," I said.

"Can you help me tie yours back on?" he asked.

He could tie the necklace himself, but he was trying to make amends. It wasn't fair of me to be mean to him, so I opened my bedroll and sat on my bent legs. He walked over to me and then sat down just in front of me, facing me. I took the necklace from his hand and put it around his neck, trying to ignore the closeness of our faces and the scent of his body.

I hadn't realized how upset I was until I tried to tie the necklace and couldn't because my hands were shaking too much. I tried again to tie it and dropped it. "Dammit," I said angrily. I reached down to pick it up, but he grabbed my hands and held them inside of his.

"Everything's going to be alright. I won't let them take you," he said seriously. I was avoiding looking at his eyes, but he tilted his head sideways and down so he could look at my face. "I'm going to protect you like I promised to twelve years ago. You don't have to be scared."

I jerked my hands away from his and quickly tied the necklace around his neck. "I'm not scared. And I don't need your protection."

He ignored me and went to his bedroll to finish eating. "I hope Macon isn't too angry. Maybe we'll get out of it because of what happened."

"Good night," I said as I wrapped myself up in my bedroll again, choosing to ignore his attempt at conversation.

"Good night," he said softly.

I knew I should have been nicer, but he'd made me mad by his niceness. Even as crazy as it was to be mad that he was nice, I was. He should have kept that comment to himself instead of telling me. I knew he would protect me because he always did. He took his word seriously and when he vowed to protect me back then, he hadn't broken it since.

For once I really hoped he would keep his word and even though I said I didn't need his protection, I truly wanted it.

I relaxed and prayed that tomorrow would be uneventful and we would make it to school easily. As the time passed, I didn't think I'd be able to fall asleep, but then Favian moved his bedroll closer to mine and with his reassuring presence so close, I fell asleep to the sound of the nocturnal creatures stirring and the crickets chirping.

A n uneventful night and an uneventful morning were good signs for us as we rode towards the school. Favian was still

being silent and I could see him scanning everything ahead to ensure our safety. I kept on high alert as well, but Favian could see and hear miles ahead of me so there truly wasn't much of a point.

The trees ended and we began passing farm land where families were already out pruning, gathering and inspecting their crops. A small girl with a dirt smeared face waved to us and Favian and I waved back.

"Momma did you see the girl fighter? I wish I could be a fight er," the girl said excitedly.

"Hush child, we mustn't keep them. Leave them be on their way," the mother said as she continued picking.

Soon the town came into view and the large wooden walls surrounding it. Favian backed up so that we were riding side by side and kept extra close to me as we approached. We were forced to stop at the closed gate and wait for the guard to grant us admission to the city.

"Who goes there?" the head guard called out from behind the walls.

"Humble students of the Academy," I called back.

"Is that little Marin?" he asked just before he popped his head up and over the top of the walls. "My, you aren't so little anymore are you girl?"

"No gatekeeper. I have grown some since I last came one month ago," I teased him.

"May we be allowed entrance?" Favian asked.

"In a hurry, are we Favian?" the gatekeeper asked with a smirk.

"We're late and the roads have not been safe," he said as a hint to the gatekeeper.

"Why didn't you say so?" the gatekeeper asked angrily. We heard him climbing down and yelling orders to the other guards and then the gate began to move inward slowly.

Favian nudged Fire's side with his leg and she trotted forward through the small opening in the gate with Ice following close behind. I turned and glared at Favian for touching my horse, but he just looked back at me. Why did he have to be so infuriating sometimes? We made it inside and the guards shut the gate quickly behind us.

"What happened on the road?" the gatekeeper asked with the other guards around.

"I'm heading to the Academy," I said bitterly.

"Just wait a second," Favian ordered. He turned

to the gatekeeper. "We were attacked by six human bandits. One of them had a picture of Marin with a note on the back to kidnap her alive and bring her."

"Kidnap Marin?" the gatekeeper asked in shock. "Who would want to do such a thing? She don't cause no harm anywhere."

"Favian, we need to go," I urged him.

"You two run on. I'll let the others know. We'll see if we can dig something up," the gatekeeper said. "And Favian, keep a close eye on her."

"He always does," I whispered bitterly as we finally trotted through town towards the other side where a few miles beyond the border of the town lie Macon Academy.

The town was busy with trading and people milled about with their goods or with their carts to purchase items. I could smell the delightful scent of cooking meat. I knew we didn't have time to stop, but I desperately wanted a bite. I vowed to come get some on our first break.

Once through the town, we were let out the back gate where the guards had already heard of our news. We galloped the last four miles to school and finally came to stand in front of the massive gates of the Academy. We both knew that if we weren't supposed to be approaching the gates, we would have been stopped by one of the six guards placed sporadically throughout the trees on the side of the road on our approach. We also knew that of the six guards, two were sleeping, one was eating and two had waved at us. The last guard had been very stealthy and I hadn't been able to spot him. Or he was away from his post.

"Ye be late," the guard said as we stood before the gates.

"Yes, Master Gatekeeper, we are late, but with good reason," I said as we waited for him to open the doors.

"There's ne'er a good reason to be late," he responded, but opened the gate and allowed us entrance. "Straight to Macon's chambers," he said. "Don't dawdle."

Favian and I trotted our horses inside and I exhaled in relief. I felt the worry ease off of my shoulders and the fears evaporate now that we were safe within the school's grounds.

The Academy had over one hundred acres of land, most of which was used for training scenarios in various conditions such as cliffs, mountain passes and forests. There were eight large buildings, Macon's office, the healer's quarters, the dorm, the armory, the blacksmith, the stable, the food hall and the covered fighting ring. There was also one very small building next to the dorm where I lived. They had not wanted me to share sleeping quarters with the males so I was forced to build my own dorm to live in. It had taken me three months and in those three months I'd slept outside on the ground until it was done. Favian had snuck out during the night to help me build, but couldn't assist me in the day when he might have gotten caught.

We stopped at Macon's office and tied our horses to the hitching post even though Fire and Ice would stand if we simply dropped their reins on the ground. We dismounted and knocked twice on the door before

Macon said, "Enter."

We stepped inside and I raised my right arm in time to block the blunt knife being stabbed towards my throat. It was standard procedure to be tested when walking inside a building where your eyesight temporarily disappeared due to the change from bright lighting to dark lighting. I knew this. I'd been tested this way hundreds of times and yet I freaked out at this attack. I elbowed my attacker and punched him in the thigh, making him drop to his knees. Favian was fighting beside me against an opponent on his left and faring better than me. I heard movement behind me, but was too slow to move to protect myself.

I braced for a hit, but Favian spun around and used the blunt knife he'd been attacked with, and had somehow gotten possession of, to smack the person attempting to attack me in their face.

"Favian!" Macon yelled angrily. "What the hell are you doing?" Favian dropped the knife and turned to face Macon who was sitting in his chair, behind his desk twenty feet in front of us watching the whole ordeal. Favian looked at me and I could tell he wanted to know if I was okay. I blinked long one time, our silent communication for yes. "I apologize, Macon and Timothy," Favian said and then bowed.

"Favian and Marin, inside. The rest of you leave us," Macon said angrily. The other guys left and shut the door behind them. I faced towards Macon and stood at attention since there was nothing else I could do until Macon gave us orders. Favian did the same beside me with a stoic face.

Macon's building consisted of two floors, the first

was Macon's office where he had his desk and chairs to meet with people and a very large fireplace that I had never seen used. The upstairs was his living quarters and none were allowed up there.

"You've been good so far at keeping your fights separate. Why did you protect her just now?" he asked Favian.

"My nerves are on edge and my protectiveness is on high alert. I apologize and will not do it again while we are inside the Academy's boundaries," Favian said.

"What happened to upset you so much that you lost your ability to protect yourself?" Macon asked me.

"We were attacked by six human bandits. We easily dispatched them, but the leader had a picture of me with a note on the back," I said softly.

Favian handed the picture to Macon. "Turn it over," he said.

Macon turned the picture over and a deep crease split the center of his forehead. "When did this happen?"

"Yesterday around the afternoon," Favian answered.

"I want a full report. Every single detail you can remember," he said sternly to Favian. "Marin, go tend to the horses and take your bags to your rooms. Once you're done with that fetch Master Sean and Master Martin and escort them to me immediately."

"Yes, sir," I said and bowed before leaving the building. I didn't like being sent off on the errands, but I knew better than to question Macon. I untied the horses from the hitching post and led them to the stables where I quickly untacked them and put our things on our specified racks. I then put the horses inside their stalls, which were thankfully already full of water and hay. I jogged to the dorms, waving to fellow students as I did and then knocked on the boys' dorm.

The door opened and Micah, one of the few who had immediately liked me despite the fact that I was a girl, opened the door. "Hey Marin. Where's Favian?"

"Busy with Macon. Can you put his bag on his bunk for me?" I asked as I tossed the bag inside the door. "Thanks!"

"You're welcome," he called to me as I jogged to my dorm and tossed my bag inside the door.

Master Sean was the weapons and hand to hand combat master and Master Martin was the archery and tactics master. If my guess was right, they were probably both at the outdoor training grounds working with students. I ran around the dorms and passed the blacksmith's building to the large sand-filled, rectangular training ground. At least fifty students filled the outer area of the arena, watching two others in the center. The students at the Academy were comprised of Humans, Goblins, a couple Dwarves, one Elf besides Favian and the occasional Sidhe, but the Sidhe kept to themselves mainly. Both Master Sean and Martin were standing near the center, watching the students and giving them pointers. Master Sean was built lean and muscular and Master Martin was built short and stocky with thick arms. They were opposites of each other and yet the best of friends.

I stepped into the ring and nodded to a few of the students before stepping passed them so the masters would be able to see me. The two students were battling intensely with short swords in the center of the ring and the masters were focused on their movements. I needed to get their attention so I called out loudly, "Masters."

Both men turned to me and then told the students to stop. "Come to spar?" Master Martin asked with a wicked smile.

"No, sirs. I have come to get you at the request of Macon. You are to accompany me immediately," I said in my serious tone.

The men looked at each other and then turned to the students. Master Sean said, "One on one training until we return. We hear of any slackers and you're running laps and doing extra guard times."

"Yes, sir!" the students said together.

I turned and the two men jogged after me towards Macon's office. I knocked on the door twice and then opened it. "They are here, sir."

"Good," Macon said from where he was pacing behind his desk. "Favian escort Marin to her dorm and stay with her until I summon you both. Masters, please sit in front of my desk."

"What's going on?" Master Sean asked. "Why the sudden call here?"

"Are we being attacked?" Martin asked with excitement. He was the only one I knew who would *want* to be attacked.

Favian and I made our exit and headed towards the dorms. "I don't need a bodyguard inside the damn grounds," I complained. I truly wanted to stay and hear what Macon had to say.

"He's just trying to take precautions and protect his student.

He'd do the same for any student," Favian said.

We walked the rest of the way in silence to my dorm and then sat in the center of the floor. "I just want to get back to training and finish up the program. I'm so close," I said softly.

"We'll get there. It's only the first day. We have three months of torture left."

I took my sword from its sheath and put it underneath my bed, reaching further underneath to take out the blunt sword we had to carry around while at the school and put it in the sheath. I hated taking off my real sword, but I had no choice here. "Three months isn't that long," I whispered.

"Are you worried about what job you will get after?" he asked.

I shrugged. "Not really. I am up for any job."

"Except being a member of the Human's army, right?"

I looked at Favian in shock. "I can't believe you even asked me that."

"Well, you are human, Marin. It does make sense that you might want to join with other humans."

Fear built up within me at his tone. "Is that what you want? Do you want me to join the humans?" I asked him quietly as I met his gaze.

Instantly, I saw the truth in his eyes and felt the twist of worry ease from my stomach. "No," he said. "Of course, I don't want you to join the Humans."

"Then we have no need to bring it up again. The only King I serve is Cesar," I said adamantly.

47

We stopped talking and sat in silence for half an hour. I knew because I counted the seconds. Favian broke the silence and asked, "Do you want to practice some magic while we wait?"

I wasn't very skilled at magic, but with Favian's help, I'd learned a few spells and incantations that were beneficial. "Sure," I said with a nod of my head.

He scooted closer to me and crossed his legs. "Put your palms face up on your knees like this." I mimicked his sitting position and did as he asked. "Now, close your eyes and take a deep calming breath." I did as he said and felt myself relax a little more. "Okay, now you remember how to find your power?" I nodded. "Good. I want you to find it and pull a small bit of it into each palm."

This was the difficult part for me. I could find the power, but it was hard for me to direct it. I kept my calm and searched within myself to find the small spark that was my magic. After finally finding it, I pictured sending bits of the spark from my heart, down my arms and into my palms. I had to picture it three times before I finally got it to work.

"Good," he said softly. "Now I want you to change that spark into a flame."

I'd never tried that before. Could I change a spark into a flame? How? I had to trust that he knew I could learn it. I took another cleansing breath and imagined the spark being changed into a flame.

Nothing happened.

I almost laughed at myself. I couldn't *change* a spark into a flame. I pictured the spark flaring into the next stage of a spark, a flame. You couldn't change an item; you had to use a catalyst or use the next stage of an item's life. I had to use a lot of strength to do it, but after a moment of straining the flame flared in my palm and I smiled victoriously.

"Good. Now pull the flame into your core where your power is and let it mix with your power."

I concentrated and slowly, but surely, pulled the flame into the spot where my power was. The instant the flames touched the spark, my body filled with power and the spark was transformed into a flame. I gasped in shock and my eyes flew open as it surged through me. Gradually the power subsided inside of me and instead of the spark which had been there, a flame flickered within me.

"How do you feel?" he asked me with a smug smile. "Wow," I whispered. "That was intense."

"Yes, but now your power will be permanently increased."

"Can you exponentially increase your power this way?" I asked him as I shook out my body, which felt tingly all over.

"How do you think Elves gain so much power? You can only do this once every two months, but as you can imagine, over time it can make you extremely powerful."

"Do other races know of this technique?" I asked him. If humans were aware of this there were bound to be many overly powerful beings.

"No. This is an Elf only technique," he said seriously.

I jerked my head up to meet his eyes. "Why did you teach me? Won't you get in trouble? I don't want you getting in trouble because of me."

He put his hand on my shoulder and met my eyes with his serious prince gaze. "You are part of the Elves. You are a favored daughter of the King and Queen, no matter your rounded ears and darker skin," he said as he lightly tugged on the top of my ear where his became pointed, but mine stayed round. "I taught you because you needed to know to increase your power and I trust that you won't teach anyone else the technique."

I felt my eyes starting to water and clenched them shut. "Thank you."

He wiped a tear that had escaped off of my face and laughed softly. "You females are so tender," he whispered.

I opened my eyes and punched him as hard as I could in the shoulder. He grunted in pain and tackled me to the ground. I rolled out from under him and we faced off. I knew I couldn't win because he was faster and stronger, but we had been sparring partners since we were kids and old habits die hard. He darted forward, trying to grab me around my waist, but I jumped up over his head, having to duck my head down so I wouldn't hit the ceiling and wrapped my arms around his neck. Unfortunately, he turned just before I did that and we ended up embracing each other with our noses touching. My cheeks flooded with blood and I jerked away from him just as someone knocked on my door.

"Enter," Favian said as I turned away from them to face the back wall and fought with my strange emotions once again.

"Macon summons you," Micah said in his fake serious tone.

Why was I embarrassed? Favian and I had hugged many times. I had shared sleeping sacks with him many times as well. Why did a close hug now make my blood pound and my head spin?

"Alright," Favian replied. I heard him walking, but was still trying to figure out the weird feelings so I had not moved yet. "Marin?"

I finally calmed my heart and got the blood to flow out of my face. "Sorry," I whispered. "I was just thinking." I turned around and followed behind them as we walked.

"How was your break?" Micah asked Favian.

Favian shrugged. "Same as always. I do my part as Prince, bowing and dancing and flirting with maidens. The only happy parts were during the nights when Marin and I snuck off to practice."

"Is she any better?" Micah asked.

"She can hear you," I said before smacking Micah in the back of the head.

Micah laughed. "I wasn't sure if she was paying attention."

"She is better, but still a slow girl," Favian teased.

"I can kick your butt. I just choose not to," I said defensively. "If I were to beat you, your reputation and title as Prince would be put in jeopardy and as your friend, I cannot allow that to happen."

Favian rolled his eyes at me and Micah laughed at us both.

We arrived at Macon's office and Micah opened the door for us. Macon waved us in and I was shocked to see all of the employees and the leaders of each of the years of students inside of the office. It was extremely cramped with so many people inside, but I made my way in and nodded at the people I hadn't had a chance to say hello to yet.

"We've just updated everyone on your situation," Macon told me. "And unfortunately, with so little information we have no way of figuring out who is after you."

"But we think we have a plan," Master Sean said. "What kind of plan?" Favian asked skeptically.

"Would you be ready for your final exam in one month instead of three?" Macon asked me.

"Yes," I said in my strong Mercenary voice.

"Good," Macon said with a smile. "Then this year's finalists will be taking their exam two months early and this will probably be the most difficult exam ever given."

"Sir, what plan do you have to find out who is after Marin?" Favian asked.

All eyes turned to him, shocked at his serious tone. I rarely heard him use the tone, usually only when ordering people around for important items when he was in Prince mode. And I'd never heard him use it on a superior before.

"We're going to use all of the finalists to stage an operation to lure out the kidnapper to apprehend them. Once apprehended, we will either get them to confess who hired them or torture them until they tell us," Macon said.

"You're going to use me as bait," I said with a smile.

Master Martin smiled back at me. "You are the best-looking bait we've got in this school."

"No," Favian said angrily. "We are not using her as bait. She could be hurt or killed. She could be kidnapped and…"

"And that is the only way that we will be able to find out who is after me," I said softly, stopping Macon from yelling at Favian's outburst. Macon's eyes glowed with fury and I knew that if I didn't defuse Favian quickly, he would take the brunt of that anger.

"Marin, I will not allow you to…" Favian began.

I turned and stared straight into his eyes. "Don't you think I'm aware that I could be killed?! You think I want to play damsel in distress when someone's not right beside me? I don't want to, but it's necessary and besides, it's my decision. I want to find out who is after me and why and if the only way to do that is to prance around the city square then dammit, I will put on a dress and prance around. I know you are worried and I appreciate it, but this is what we are trained for. You have to trust your brothers to be able to help us. Most of all, we have to do this or we won't graduate."

"Father won't allow it," he said giving me his cold stare.

I hated the cold stare. It meant that he was mad at me and wouldn't talk to me for the next day or two. "Father does not need to know what we are planning. You can apprise him of our encounter and leave it at that."

"This is ridiculous," he said. "Does no one but me value your life?"

"You've crossed a line with those words," Macon

said dangerously angry.

"You are all mad," Favian said and then stormed out of the office.

I'd never heard of anyone walking out of Macon's office without permission. I turned and Macon waved his hand dismissively. "Leave him be."

"Why wait a month?" I asked him. "Why can't we do this sooner?"

"We need to plan everything out and be sure that we can protect you during this operation."

"I can protect myself," I reminded him.

Macon smiled. "We are all aware of your capabilities, Marin. We are not belittling them, but I will not put a student in any type of danger which could possibly end with your death. After you leave these grounds, then you can do as many dangerous jobs as you like."

"If they had wanted me dead, they would have told them to kill me, not kidnap me alive."

"Perhaps whoever it is wants to kill you themselves," Micah suggested.

"That is a possibility," Master Sean agreed.

"So, for the next month the Masters and I will plan the operation out while you work your hardest on your close combat and escape maneuvers. You'll need everything you've been taught during this final," Macon said. "For now, all of you go eat lunch."

All of the students who had been sitting stood up and everyone saluted Macon. "Yes, sir," we said in unison.

I walked out the door and Micah walked beside me. "This is exciting, isn't it?"

"Yes, my upcoming kidnapping and probable death is very exciting," I said sarcastically.

"Oh, come on. You know you'll be safe," he said with a smile. "Come on we need to find Favian for lunch," I replied to change the subject.

"Any idea where he is?" he asked.

I smiled. "I know exactly where he is." We jogged around the dorms and I led Micah to the outdoor training ground. As soon as we were within ear shot, we heard the yells of several males battling and when it came into view, I could see Favian battling with six other students.

We walked up to the arena and I stepped inside, moving out into the ring so he would see me. The six fighting Favian were other finalists and some of the toughest students in the school. Favian ducked a punch from two of them at once and then darted forward to punch a third in the face before he could pull his sword from his belt. I watched Favian's speed and grace and smiled at his flawless form.

When Favian was focused, no one could beat him. I however knew his one weakness. Fortunate for me his weakness happened to be *me*. The six students were tired and I could see they were beginning to falter. If I didn't intercede soon, one of them would get injured by Favian's anger. I stepped around one of the students and pulled my sword from my sheath. Favian spun around, hearing the sword drawn and stopped with his sword a fraction of an inch from mine. "Blowing off some steam?" I asked.

He pulled his sword back and took a step back. "I hate when you do that."

"Macon ordered all of us to lunch. Let's go before you get in trouble for your rudeness earlier and disobeying him now," I said and took a step back.

"I'm not hungry," he said as he turned towards a new student who had replaced one of the tired ones.

I darted forward and sliced at Favian's back. He spun around and blocked my blade with his. "Macon has summoned everyone for lunch. All of you need to leave." The other students grumbled, but left, including Micah, leaving Favian and I alone. I waited until everyone was out of ear shot and said, "Talk to me."

Favian sheathed his sword and headed out of the arena. "It's lunch time."

I grabbed his arm and turned him back towards me, but he wouldn't look at me. "Don't ignore me," I said angrily. "We're partners remember?"

"What good is a partner if they will not listen to you?" he asked bitterly before pulling out of my hold and walking away.

He'd never been so angry with me before. Didn't he understand that I was scared? That I didn't want to risk my life even though I knew I needed to? How could he abandon me when I needed him at my back the most?

I walked numbly to the food hall finding it out of habit instead of sight and walked inside. Everyone was already eating and talking so I made my way up the line and got food quickly. There were very few people who didn't like a girl being at the Academy, so I could sit with anyone, but I usually sat with Favian and Micah. With Favian being so mad at me though,

I didn't want to sit with him or anyone else. I carried my tray with a bowl of soup and chunk of bread and sat at the single empty table where I had spent my first two weeks when I'd originally come to the Academy. I could have sat with Favian when I had first come here, but I had been trying to give him time to make friends with some of the males and so I had sat alone.

Sitting at the table again made me feel alone and sad for the first time since I'd come here six years ago. Several pairs of eyes were turned towards me as people gossiped about the rumors and what they had found out so far. The only pair of eyes averted from me were Favian's. I wanted to cry and yell at him at the same time. I ate my food with my eyes cast down and ignored anyone who came near me in an attempt to talk. Things were going fine until Brian came to my table.

Brian was tall with dark hair and eyes and a perpetually foul demeanor. "You and your boyfriend having a fight?" he asked with a sneer.

"I'm not in the mood, Brian," I said before taking a bite of my bread.

"It must be hard to have him mad at you and not be able to run to him for affection. I'm willing to show you some affection if you're lonely," he said as he reached towards me.

I slapped his hand away and stood up. All eyes turned to us. "Touch me and I'll stab you," I said venomously.

"I'm just offering my services to a needy damsel," he said smugly and then reached for my bread.

No one takes food from each other in the hall. It is a rule that is strictly enforced and one that you are allowed to punish the person for. I pulled my knife and stabbed his hand to the table before he reached my bread. "That is my food. If you're hungry then I suggest you return to your table and finish yours." I jerked my blade from his hand and cleaned it on the bottom of my cloak.

He didn't make a sound of pain, but I could tell he was hurting. Being stabbed always hurt. He raised his hand to hit me and the chef threw his ladle into the back of Brian's head. "You try to steal her food again and I'll tie you up to the post," chef said angrily. "Return to your seat or leave if you're done."

Brian glared at me and I said, "You know the rules. Keep your hands to yourself unless we're sparring just as you do to the males here."

"I hope you do get kidnapped. It would serve you right for sullying the Academy with your presence," he said and then spat on my shirt.

Now he had pissed me off. I punched him as hard as I could in the face with my right hand and then punched him in the stomach with my left hand. He doubled over and I kneed him in the face at the same time I made a fist with both hands and hit him in the back. The students were cheering loudly and standing up to see the battle better.

As I moved to knock him out Master Sean grabbed me around the waist and pulled me back. "I'm impressed," he said. "You put quite a bit of force into those moves."

"Let me go and I'll impress you some more," I said

as I pulled against him.

Brian stood up and wiped blood from underneath his nose. "You'll pay for that."

"Pay for what? Kicking your butt fair and square?" Micah asked. "You should have kept your spit in your mouth and she wouldn't have hit you."

"Shut your mouth. We all know you want her," Brian said with a scowl at Micah.

Micah stepped up to Brian and smiled in his face. "Care to go outside and see who can back up their words with their fists? You've already been embarrassed by Marin. Do you really want to be embarrassed by me as well?"

"Let me finish teaching him a lesson," I begged Master Sean. "He doesn't know when to shut his mouth and I desperately want to teach him."

"Save your strength. You and I are to spar after lunch," he said. *I was going to spar with a master!* "Eat your lunch and meet me in the covered arena. Brian, follow me."

He released me and then waited for Brian to walk past me and out the door. I sat down on the bench and used the bottom of my cloak to wipe the spit off my shirt. My poor cloak was in desperate need of a washing after only one day.

"You alright?" Micah asked.

"Fine," I said as I resumed eating my soup and bread.

Micah set a mug of water on the table in front of me. "You always forget your water."

"Thanks," I said as I took a drink. "And thanks for defending me, but you know you don't need to do that."

Micah shrugged. "I'm tired of his cocky attitude anyways. I really wish I could have taken him outside." He watched me eat for a second and then asked, "Why are you eating alone?"

"He's mad at me," I whispered so that Favian couldn't hear me. "You guys are best friends and partners. He'll get over it. And plus, that is no reason for you to eat alone."

I finished my meal and picked my bowl up to take to the bin where the chef would clean them later. "Thanks, but I've got to go." Favian was standing up and looked like he might have been waiting for me, but I kept my eyes forward and walked by him without a glance in his direction. If he wanted to be mad, two could play that game. I walked from the food hall to the covered arena and shoved all of my girly emotions down inside where they belonged.

It was an honor to spar with one of the masters and the thought made me giddy and nervous at the same time. I climbed over the railing and dropped down into the dirt arena where Master Sean *and* Master Martin were standing together talking.

"Masters," I said with a bow.

Master Martin smiled. "I'm sure you're nervous having the both of us here, but due to your circumstances we are going to be giving you extra lessons with sparring against us to better prepare you for the final."

He called it a final like it was a normal test. Like my life wasn't in danger. Would I become so callous when I was their age?

"Today we are going to teach you quick techniques which will help you get out of situations where you might be tied up," Master Martin said as he uncoiled a rope.

"So, you're going to tie me up and teach me how to get untied?" I asked to clarify.

Master Martin smiled. "Exactly."

I did not like the gleam in his eyes. It was a frightening gleam, but I knew there was nothing I could do to stop it and I also knew that he was simply trying to teach me how to save my own life. Or at least I hoped that was the reason they were teaching me this.

"Okay," I said with a nod of my head, "Let's get started."

Four hours later my arms, legs, wrists, ankles, throat, and hands were covered in rope burns and bruises and my skills

had barely improved. They promised to write down my new schedule and have it delivered to me before lights out. Apparently, I was going to have more private lessons and a much longer day than the others. I limped into the food hall and stood in line for food with the other students and wished for some of the pain medicine that Mother kept on hand for me at the castle. It was instant relief and always made me feel happy.

"You look like crap," Micah said with a laugh.

"Thanks," I muttered as I limped forward in line.

"Training with the Masters one on one not exactly what you dreamed it would be?"

I shrugged and then grunted in pain from the movement. "It's intense, but I can handle it." Favian was behind Micah, but he was still mad at me and ignoring me so I did the same to him. "How were your training sessions?" I asked Micah.

He shrugged. "Not much new. We basically recapped everything we learned before we left for break so that they could be sure we remembered everything."

"I practiced throughout break so I'm glad I missed that. I would have been bored," I said. I grabbed a bowl and held it out for the chef to pour soup in.

He smiled. "You look mighty beat up, girl. Don't forget your water this time."

"Yes, sir," I said with a nod as I moved down and grabbed a piece of bread. I grabbed a mug of water and made my way to the empty table and sat down.

"Marin, come sit with us," Micah said from the table we usually sat at.

"No thanks," I said and then turned away from everyone and ate my food.

"You can't stay mad at her forever," Micah said to Favian. "Don't make her eat alone."

"She makes her own choices," Favian said angrily. "You two are so stubborn," Micah complained.

Lucias and Lucian sat down at my table with duplicate green-skinned, sharp toothed smiles. They were identical twin Goblins who always tried to confuse people on who was who and most of the time they succeeded. Luckily, I had figured out the one difference between the two and was able to identify them. "Hello Lucian," I said to the one on the right with the slightly larger ears. "Hello Lucias," I said to the one on the left.

"She always gets it right," Lucian complained.

"It's no fun." Lucias smiled. "We come bearing gifts."

That made me very suspicious. Goblins did not bear gifts freely. "What's the catch?"

"No catch," they said in unison.

I folded my arms across my chest. "There's always a catch."

Lucian said, "We see the Elf is angry and you're not speaking and we see the bruises and burns. Plus, you're the only one who knows us apart and we appreciate it so we want to be friendly and give you a gift. No catch."

"Here," Lucias said as he slid a leather pouch across the table. "It has healing medicine and pain relief in it."

"No catch?" I asked again.

They smiled and Lucias said, "You're nice and we like nice people. No catch."

I took the pouch and smiled at them. "Thank you."

"You're welcome," they said in unison and then stood up and walked out of the building. How did it not bother them to speak in unison? I would be slapping my sibling if they tried that with me. Not that I had any siblings, but if I did, I wouldn't let them mimic me.

After finishing my food, I limped out of the food hall to my dorm and collapsed onto my bed. I needed to put the medicines the goblin twins had given me on, but I was too exhausted to move anymore. Someone knocked on my door and I groaned. Couldn't I get ten minutes of peace?

"Enter," I called out, refusing to get up and go to the door.

Favian stepped inside and I glared at him. "Exit."

He shut the door behind him and sat down on the bed beside me. "What did the goblins want with you?"

"To barter for my body for a night of pleasure," I said angrily. "Get out of my dorm." I tried to sit up, but every movement hurt and I gave up.

"What did they really want?" he asked.

"Are you listening to me? I want you to leave," I said, this time using my anger to force myself up. I started to walk to the door, but he grabbed my forearm to stop me. My burns and bruises made me yell out in pain and drop to my knees.

"Why didn't you tell me you were in so much pain?" he asked angrily as he released me and began inspecting my wounds.

I slapped his hands away and used the bed to stand up. "Get out. I don't want to see you."

He growled angrily and stood up. "Fine, don't tell me what they wanted. I'll go talk to them myself."

I turned my back to him and opened the leather pouch the goblins had given me. Inside was the healing medicine in a small wooden tube and the pain reliever in a clear container. My door opened and closed as Favian left and I was alone again. I opened the healing medicine and spread it onto one burn, holding my breath to see if it would sting or not. Surprisingly, it didn't sting and it gave me immediate relief. I stripped out of my clothes and spread the medicine everywhere I had bruises and burns and then put a small amount of the white powder pain reliever on my tongue and let it dissolve. My pain vanished and I felt invigorated again. I was definitely going to have to get the twins a present for this!

After redressing and hiding the medicines in the pouch in the bottom of my bag, I headed out to the outdoor training arena for a meeting with Master Martin. As I neared it, I realized this was not a meeting, but a set up. The arena was filled with every student of the school and every teacher was there as well, sitting up on the railings. I stepped inside the arena and Master Martin waved me forward. I walked to him, looking at all of the faces around until I spotted the one I was seeking. I immediately turned away from him, having only been wondering if he was there.

"Marin, I'm glad you made it. Did the earlier training make you sore?" Master Martin asked.

"Yes," I said in a truthful statement. The training had made me sore, but the medicine the twins gave me had cured that.

"I'm sure you'll loosen up soon."

"What's going on?" I asked him. "Why is everyone here?"

"Today is a trial," Macon said as he stepped into the arena. "A trial?" I asked in shock. "Against me?"

"More of a trial because of you," he answered with a smirk.

"I do not understand," I replied. "Why a trial? What is to be proved?"

"Those my dear, are the perfect questions. We are putting on trial whether females should be allowed to join the Academy more often than just your case," Macon said as he walked to the center of the ring.

Now I understood. I was the first female to be allowed to attend, let alone complete the Academy.

They had to test me to see if it was a good idea to allow females to attend in the future. "I understand," I said with a nod of my head. "What trials am I to face?" This was so sudden and seemingly random. Had Favian known? Was that why he had really come to my dorm?

"You'll be tested in everything," Macon said. "But first, we will test you on your fighting skills." Macon nodded at Master Sean.

Master Sean smiled evilly at me and then snapped his fingers. Two first year students climbed down from the railing and approached me. I pushed my cloak back behind me and gave myself freedom of movement depending upon the type of attack they used on me. "Hand to hand, no weapons," Master Sean instructed. "Begin!"

The two boys charged me and I forgot about the kidnapping attempt. I forgot about Favian being mad at me. I forgot about everything except the trial. I would prove that females should be allowed. I would prove that I was a capable Mercenary and I would prove that I could be a Protector. The newbies charged forward enthusiastically and I ducked their wild swings easily and kicked them in the backs to use their own momentum against them. They both stumbled forward and down to their hands and knees and then jumped up and turned towards me again. I took a wide stance and put my hands in defensive positions near my face.

The boys moved away from each other so that they would both come at me from different sides and then darted towards me again. I blocked and punched and kicked and after only a minute had them both on the ground, knocked out.

I backed away from them so others could drag them out of the arena and faced Master Sean waiting for his next signal. "Swords," he said and then snapped his fingers. Two second year students hopped down and drew their swords. I drew mine and fought to keep the smile off of my face. I knew it was a test, yet I felt no fear or worry, only cheerfulness.

Master Sean yelled, "Begin!"

The two looked at each other and then one of them ran at me. I blocked his downward thrust and elbowed him in the stomach before rolling away from the second guy's sword. He spun around in an advanced technique no second year should have known and I barely had time to jump back from the blade which skimmed passed my shirt. I sliced upward, catching him in the chin and knocked him on his back.

"That's why you don't use advanced techniques until you learn them," Micah called teasingly.

The student still standing circled me and I stood loose and ready for his attack. "You're not as good as you think you are," he said bitterly.

"I never said I was good," I answered seriously.

"Your confident attitude says it for you."

I smiled. "I'm not confident, just calm and prepared for anything you throw at me."

He snarled and kicked sand up at my face, trying to blind me. I dashed backwards and wiped at my eyes trying to see him before he got within striking distance. The crowd booed and I heard Master Sean curse angrily. I finally got the sand out of my eyes and found the boy circling me silently. I pretended to still be blind and swung wildly with my sword in the opposite direction as the boy. He smiled smugly and dashed forward, expecting to catch me off guard from his dirty play. I spun around and blocked his blow, elbowing him in the face at the same time and then pressed my sword to his throat. "Cheap tricks don't work," I said with a smile.

"You're a fool," Master Sean said. "And an embarrassment for using such a dirty trick."

I finished wiping my eyes out and faced Master Sean. "Third years?" I guessed.

He smiled. "Yes. Multiple opponents."

"Wonderful," I said as four muscular kids climbed down from the railing.

The kids spread out to form a square around me and took loose, ready stances. They were obviously better trained than the other kids I'd fought so far, but that made sense because they were third years. "Begin," Master Sean said.

Unlike before, no one moved. I turned slowly to be able to look at everyone as they kept their cool in statue stances. I took a deep breath and then they moved at once. I couldn't think of moves ahead of time because they attacked too quickly. In what seemed like an hour, but was really only a couple of minutes, I finally defeated all of them. I leaned over, taking deep breaths and trying to calm myself. My heart was beating faster than normal and a weird fire burned inside of me at the exhilaration of the fighting.

"Whoa," one of the students on the railing said. "I didn't even see how she did that."

Students walked out to help the third years off of the sand and to tend to the few cuts I'd opened when punching them.

"Fourth year," Master Sean called. "Archery."

Finally, I could take a break from fighting. I sheathed my sword and squatted down to rest my legs a bit. I wasn't very good at archery, so this test had me the most nervous. I could handle myself in a fight, but standing still and aiming at a target one hundred yards away was not my strong suit.

Master Martin walked out into the arena and handed me a bow and quiver of arrows. "Do your best."

"I always do," I said as I positioned the quiver on my back and faced the target which had been placed at the other end of the arena.

A tall skinny guy whom I'd met, but couldn't remember his name, walked out with a bow and quiver to stand next to me. He held out his hand with a smile. "I'm Tristan. Good luck, Marin."

I smiled and shook his hand. "Same to you, Tristan."

He took an arrow out and aimed carefully. I found myself holding my breath with him and for some reason actually rooting for him. Had I injured my brain during my training?

He released the string and the arrow whizzed down the arena. A few of the students whistled in appreciation and then several cheered as the arrow hit the perfect center of the target.

"Well, hell," I whispered. "I'm not going to be able to top that."

I aimed carefully and released the bow's string. The arrow sailed down the arena and landed two inches to the right of Tristan's. A couple kids laughed and others clapped encouragingly.

Tristan shrugged. "You're close. You tilt your shoulder when you release your string. Try focusing on keeping your body completely still, like stone and you'll do better."

We moved over to the second target and Tristan easily hit the center of the target again. I tried to use his advice and focused on keeping my body as still as a statue, but I still missed the center by at least an inch. "Stage two," Master Martin said as students took the targets out and then made piles of wool and twine balls. The balls were used for moving targets, something I was even worse at then regular target practice.

Tristan knocked an arrow and nodded. "Ready." The students at the other end of the arena tossed up two targets and faster than I'd ever been able to, he shot the first arrow, grabbed a second from the quiver and shot the second, striking both targets before they hit the ground.

I whistled in appreciation. "That was incredible. You're really fast," I said seriously.

"Thanks," he said with a smile.

I took two arrows from my quiver and Tristan looked at me like I was crazy. I held the arrows in one hand and the bow in the other and nodded at the students. "Ready."

They tossed the targets up and I put both arrows on the bow at once, turned my bow sideways so that it was parallel with the ground and shot. The arrows hit both the targets and the students cheered.

"That was an interesting way to shoot," Tristan said teasingly.

I shrugged. "It's the easiest way for me to hit two targets close to each other. That technique does not work for more than two or for others far away from each other."

"I'll have to remember to try that sometime," he said. The students grabbed three targets and Tristan nodded. "Ready." They tossed the targets up and with the same speed and skill that he had been displaying, he hit all of the targets.

I was truly outmatched. I pulled two arrows from the quiver again and then pulled a third and held it in my teeth. "Ready!" I yelled around the arrow in my mouth. Now everyone was looking at me like I was crazy. They tossed the targets up and I hit the first two and then pulled the arrow from my mouth and aimed at the third target, but it was too close to the students and I wasn't a good enough aim. I lowered my bow and shrugged. "Like I said, that technique doesn't work all the time."

Tristan held out his hand to me again. "Good try."

I shook his hand. "Good job. I'm impressed with your archery."

Master Martin took the bow and quiver and shook his head at me. "You really need to practice your archery. You haven't improved since you were a fourth year."

"I know," I said as I rolled my neck.

Master Sean called, "Fifth year. Dual wielding weapons."

Micah tossed me a second blunt sword and gave me two thumbs up. I smiled at him and spun the blades to get accustomed to them. Dual wielding was one of my strong points, so I was actually looking forward to this trial. I walked to the center of the ring and was shocked to see Christopher walk out to me. He was a fifth year, but he usually hung out with Favian, Micah, and me during meals and was a really good guy. I had no idea he was the best skilled at dual wielding for his year.

He bowed to me and then held up his weapons in a salute. "I'm not going to go easy on you," he said seriously. "This is a test and to properly test you I must fight with all of my skill and might."

I saluted him with my weapons and said, "I would expect nothing less and know that I will not go easy on you either." We backed up two paces and then I nodded at him. He charged forward with a war cry to make any master happy and swung his swords. I parried and blocked and we made our way around the arena as he attacked. I watched his movements, waiting for an opening where I could attack him, but none were showing. I blocked high and then cut low, but he swung one of his blades around and down and blocked me. I tried to attack him again, but received a hit on my shoulder for my troubles. I jumped back and rotated my shoulder to be sure it wasn't broken and I could still fight and then jumped forward, attacking with everything that I had.

He spun around and nearly caught me in the side of the head, but I ducked at just the right moment and hit him in the stomach with the pommel of my sword before rolling to the right and hitting his lower leg. He swung down at me and I rolled away just in time to avoid his blade. I jumped up and he came at me, one side high and one low. I blocked both and spun around him to put my blade against his lower back and throat. "I win," I whispered.

"Never let her get that close to you when she's dual wielding," Master Sean said. "She's famous for her spins of death."

Christopher saluted me with his swords and I saluted him back. "Well done," he said as he limped out of the arena.

Micah walked out to me to take his sword back and said, "That was good, but you were open several times. If Christopher hadn't been so focused on getting a solid blow in, he could have nicked you several times and caused you a lot of pain."

"Good thing for me that he didn't see the openings," I whispered as my shoulder began to throb. I pulled my shirt down and was shocked to see a three-inch-long gash in my shoulder, bleeding slowly down my arm. "Ouch," I whispered.

"Sixth year. Final combat," Master Sean called. "Marin, you shouldn't continue..." Micah began.

I glared at him and pulled my shirt up. "Keep quiet. I only have one test left." He didn't want to let me continue, I could see it on his face. "Go," I said angrily. He frowned irritably, but walked to the railing and climbed up to sit on top of it. I turned and stared in absolute shock at Favian standing in the center of the ring watching me. "What exactly is final combat?" I asked Master Sean.

"It's a test to find your weakness. You fight with any weapons and the only rule is no killing." That did not make me feel any better. "Begin!" he yelled.

I could feel the blood beginning to run down my arm to my elbow, but I had to forget about that. I had to forget about everything and fight Favian. Fighting him was not easy when I was in top shape. Fighting him with my emotions on edge and my body injured was going to be downright impossible. I had to do it though. I had to prove that I could be a Mercenary, that I could attack my best friend if I had to. I took a ready stance and raised my hand, crooking one finger and moving it towards me to tell him to come at me.

He looked at me with cold eyes and for the first time I felt afraid of him. He was looking at me like we weren't friends. He was looking at me like he didn't care if he hurt me or not. He was looking at me like he didn't know who I was. The energy I had felt before and the fire I had inside turned to ice at the look in his eyes.

He charged forward and I ducked his first punch and kicked at his legs, but he sidestepped and my kick missed. I wanted to use my sword, but I was right-handed and the wound on my shoulder would only hinder my sword fighting abilities so I couldn't use it. Favian continued to press me and fight me and it was all I could do to ward off his blows.

I needed to attack him. I needed to fight back, but I couldn't. I had my throwing knives, but they weren't dulled and technically I wasn't supposed to be carrying them anyways.

Master Sean *had* said any weapons though. I was

about to pull one of them out when two spears were thrown into the center of the arena and I knew what I could do. I dodged Favian's attack and ran around him and towards the center. He was right on my heels, but I snatched up a spear before he caught up to me and spun around in a perfect arch, brought the spear up and hit him in the head.

Or I would have if he hadn't grabbed a spear as well and blocked me. I tried my hardest to hit him or cut him, but he was too skilled at everything for me to land a shot. I thought I was out of options until I saw that he was dropping his left shoulder, something his father constantly nagged him about. I watched for it again and then arched the spear up high and brought it down to slice his shoulder.

He grunted in pain and I almost smiled victoriously. It was a good thing I hadn't smiled because he swung his spear low and knocked my legs out from under me. As I fell onto my back, I only had a moment to wonder if he would hold back and then he was on top of me, trying to pin my arms with his legs. I punched his thighs and stomach and tried to get out from under him, but he was too strong.

I growled in frustration and rolled over so that my back was to him and when he leaned forward to grab my shoulders I swung my head backwards, head butting him in the face. He grunted in pain and fell backwards off of me. I spun around with my throwing knife in hand to press it to his neck, but he already had his knife out against my throat with a look of pure rage on his face.

We squatted in perfect silence with my knife's tip

against the side of his neck and the side of his blade against the front of my throat. Fear and sadness made me quiver as we held our squatted poses. It would have made for a magnificent painting had an artist been around.

We had never fought like this before. He had never come at me in anger before. I had never seen such cold eyes directed at me.

"Looks like it's a draw," Master Sean said happily with a smile.

Neither Favian nor I moved. I *couldn't* move. I couldn't look at his face. I couldn't be angry or sad. I couldn't do anything, but shake in fear as my best friend held his knife to my throat. Would this be what came of us? Would we end up killing each other in the future?

Slowly his knife was pulled away and so I pulled mine away as well.

"You're bleeding," Favian said in his normal worried voice. He reached out towards me, but I backed away from him, keeping my eyes downcast to avoid looking at anything but his face. I pulled my shirt down to expose the wound as Master Sean came towards us.

Master Sean examined the wound and frowned at me. "You should have told me you were injured after your fight with Christopher. Go to the healing building."

"Have I passed the trial?" I asked as I started walking out of the arena.

"The Masters and I are going to discuss your performance and I will let you know tomorrow,"

Macon said as he walked beside me towards the healing building. "You did well though. I'm proud of you."

"Thank you, sir," I said. I was truly happy to receive such praise from Macon. It was a high honor.

Macon pushed open the door and the healer, a short man with thick glasses looked at me and smiled. "I figured ye would be here soon. What did you make bleed this time?" I sat down on the examination table and pulled my arm out of my shirt so he could get a good look at the wound. He scoffed. "That little scratch is what brought you in here? Usually, you won't come here unless your arm is hanging out of the socket or cut in a billion pieces."

"I was ordered to come here," I said quietly.

"Ah, that explains it then." He went to work cleaning the wound and then started stitching it up. I hissed in pain a few times, but managed to hold it in so as not to appear as weak as I truly was. In truth, I wanted to cry uncontrollably from the pain of the stitches and the pain at the fight with Favian. I felt alone and I didn't like it at all.

"All done," he said. "Now go to bed."

"Yes, sir," I said as I put my arm back in my shirt and walked out of the healing building. Students were milling about, trying to have a little bit of fun before we were ordered to our quarters for the night. Some gave me thumbs up while others glared at me. I ignored them all.

Several of the other students congratulated me or told me good job, but none of it mattered. I made it to my dorm and stepped inside to find Favian sitting on my bed. I immediately turned around and headed towards the stables.

"Marin!" he called after me. "Wait."

I ignored him, trying my hardest to hold in the tears that I had been holding in since the fight. I only wanted to go to my dorm, bury my face in the pillow and let the tears flow. Now I couldn't even do that. I was almost to the stable when he grabbed my arm and stopped me. I turned my face away and tried to hide the tears falling down my face. "Release me," I said quietly.

He released my arm and I bolted around him back to my dorm. My only hope was that I would be able to lock the door before he could get in.

Sadly, I didn't have good luck. He stepped into my room and closed and locked the door behind him, trapping me inside. I sat down on my bed and calmed myself by taking deep breaths to stop my tears.

He squatted down in front of me and wiped my face. "Why are you running from me? What have I done to upset you so?"

How could I answer that? I couldn't say that he'd frightened me and hurt my feelings, could I? I couldn't tell him that I felt alone. Fresh tears spilled from my eyes and he whispered, "Tell me what you are thinking and feeling, please."

"Swear not to laugh?" I asked softly. "Of course," he said seriously.

"You're mad at me and not talking to me and then when we fought you looked at me like you didn't know me. You looked at me with cold eyes and like you didn't care if you hurt me or not."

"I frightened you," he guessed.

"Yes. I was shaking and I couldn't look at you. I couldn't see your cold eyes directed at me. It was like you weren't my friend anymore."

"I was ordered to do that," he whispered.

"I feel so alone and scared. I am scared because I could die next month and I don't want to die. I'm scared because I feel like I'm losing you and if I lose you..."

Favian wrapped his arms around me and hugged me against his chest. "I'm sorry, Marin."

The damn tears wouldn't stop coming and as I wrapped my arms around him, they turned into hard, body shaking sobs. Why was this happening? Why was my life changing so much?

He held me while I cried and then wiped my cheeks once the tears had stopped. "You aren't losing me," he whispered. "I'm sorry that I was so upset with you, but it was only because I am worried about your safety. And I am very sorry that I frightened you."

I relaxed against him and said, "I'm sorry I got emotional."

"Don't apologize for being female," he said as he released me so that he could face me on the bed. "You should have told me you were feeling this way."

I wiped my cheeks more and then grabbed the leather pouch the goblin twins had given me.

"What's that?" he asked.

"What Lucias and Lucian gave me," I answered as I pulled out the pain medication and put some on my tongue.

"Is that how you healed your rope burns so

quickly?" he asked as he took the medicines to examine them.

"Yes," I answered. "Otherwise, I would have gotten slaughtered at the trial today." The trial worried me. I had no way of knowing if I passed. I had done well, but that didn't necessarily mean they would agree to allow more females in. Not that I cared if more females were allowed in or not. Truthfully, I only cared if I graduated. "How do you think the trial went?"

"It's hard to say," he answered me honestly. "But you did very well. I was surprised you beat the first years so easily though."

I punched his arm and laughed. "Shut up."

He laughed and then met my eyes. "Are we okay?"

I shrugged. "Are we?"

He smiled and then his serious face was back and he reached forward and grabbed my chin to force me to stare into his eyes as he met mine. "My number one mission is to protect you, do you understand? I will never stop being your friend and I will protect your life with my own. I'm sorry I frightened you, but you must know that I would never hurt you, even if I was mad at you."

My heart was fluttering in that new weird way and my eyes kept dropping to his lips as he talked. Why? What was happening to me? I met his eyes again and then wrapped my arms around him to keep from kissing him like one part of my brain was telling me to do. "Thank you."

Someone knocked on the door and I jerked away from him in surprise. Favian walked to the door and unlocked it. "Enter."

Micah walked in and held out a piece of paper towards me. "Your new schedule."

I took it and groaned. "I have training with Masters Martin and Sean before the morning wakeup call and training after dinner."

"They want to be sure you are fully prepared," Favian said bitterly.

"Favian," I whispered. "I know you don't like this idea…"

He shook his head and smiled. "Don't worry about it. I trust Macon." He meant the words, but I could sense he wasn't being completely honest when he said them about this instance. "Oh, I sent word to Father so we should be hearing back from him shortly."

"Lights out!" the blacksmith yelled from his workshop. "Goodnight," Micah said. "And good luck tomorrow."

"Thanks, I think I'm going to need it," I said with a bitter laugh.

"You're alright?" Favian asked.

I nodded and smiled. "Yes."

He smiled back. "Good. I'll see you at breakfast." I walked him to the door and then locked it so that no one could sneak inside. I wasn't afraid of being kidnapped inside the Academy's grounds, but I was afraid of people playing pranks on me. I'd had it happen a couple of times and learned that you cannot get berry juice out of shirts after they've been soaked overnight. I'd had to wear a purple shirt for the rest of that semester, which had irritated the Masters more than me. I lay down and hoped I slept well since

I would need all of the energy possible to make it through the next day.

"You have to get out of the ropes without tightening the ones around your throat," Master Sean said as I struggled to do that very thing. "If you struggle too much then you will end up choking yourself until you pass out, or completely cutting off your blood supply and killing yourself."

"I'm trying," I said through clenched teeth. I wiggled my left hand and finally got the first loop over my wrist. The rest was easy and I was soon out of the ropes completely. "Yes!" I said happily.

"Good job," Master Martin said. "Your next objective is to get out of that situation in less than thirty seconds."

"Thirty seconds?!" I asked in shock. "Is that even possible?" Master Martin smiled. "My record is fifteen seconds."

That was simply amazing and ludicrous at the same time. I straightened my spine and nodded

"Alright, then I'll learn to do it in ten seconds."

Master Martin smiled and patted me on the back. "That a girl! Let's get to work."

I stood still as the two Masters tied me up and then helped me sit on the ground, completely immobile. I recalled all of the advice they had been giving me and then nodded. "Okay, start the count."

"Go," Master Martin said.

I wiggled my hand slowly and precisely, being mindful of the rope around my throat which tightened if I wiggled too much. The rope around my right wrist slid down slightly, but wasn't far enough.

"Ten seconds."

I struggled harder and faster and the rope moved farther down my wrist, but the rope around my throat was tightening… and I blacked out.

I woke up and the Masters were laughing as they finished untying me. "We told you not to move too much."

I took a deep breath and tried to clear my foggy mind. "I know."

The bell sounded for breakfast and for the first time I wanted to stay in training longer. "Go eat and attend your other trainings. After dinner, we will work on this more," Master Sean said.

I knew better than to question them or beg them to reconsider, so I bowed to them and walked towards the food hall. At least I wasn't as sore and rope burned as I had been the previous day. The lessons were working and I was learning a lot in a short amount of time.

The hall was crowded as everyone stood in line to get their breakfast. I felt irritated that they were all whining for food when they hadn't even had to train yet. My frustration grew as the line moved slowly forward and my hunger continued to gnaw at my belly.

"Marin," Favian called. I looked around the room for him, finally spotting him sitting down at a table with Micah. He waved me over and I shook my head and pointed towards the line. I hadn't gotten my food yet, why would I leave the line? He held up an extra bowl of oatmeal and smiled at me.

I walked quickly over to him and took the bowl. "Thank you," I said seriously and then began stuffing my face.

"How's training?" Micah asked.

"No talk, just eat," I said around the food in my mouth.

Favian slid my bread roll and a mug of water over in front of me. "Slow down or you'll upset your stomach."

"Yes, father," I said between gulps of oatmeal.

"How did you know I was here if you hadn't seen me?" Father asked.

I jerked my head up and stared in shock at the Elf King standing in the doorway of the food hall.

Favian stood up quickly and walked to him. "Father, I did not know you were coming."

Father sat down across the table from me. "How could I not come when I heard Marin was in danger?"

I stopped with the spoon halfway to my mouth and smiled. "I'm safe here."

He patted my hand. "We'll talk after you finish eating. You're obviously very hungry."

I nodded and went back to eating my bread and oatmeal. I was interrupted again when Mother walked inside the hall and every male turned to gawk at her. She found me and hurried over, sitting down beside me and hugging me. "Marin," she whispered.

I fought the tears that wanted to come at her show of affection and Father noticed my issue. "Amadis, let the poor girl eat. We will talk with her afterwards. Favian, we will be at Macon's office. Come there when Marin is done."

"Yes, sir," Favian said as he sat down next to me again. Mother kissed my cheek and then patted Favian's cheek before following her husband out of the food hall.

"That was fun," I whispered before tilting my bowl of oatmeal up to eat the last little bit. I was glad Mother had left because if she had seen me using such poor table manners, she would have chastised me. I could have not stood the embarrassment and teasing from the others had they witnessed that. I chugged the water in my mug and then picked up the bread roll. "We better head over before Mother threatens Macon for his plan."

"Was that the Elven King and Queen?" Micah asked in shock. I nodded. "Yep."

"She's incredibly beautiful," Micah said.

Favian rolled his eyes. "Yes, she is. Come on Marin."

I followed him out of the room with the sound of gossip behind us. I was truly shocked both of our parents had come to the Academy and also honored even though I wouldn't admit that to anyone.

We knocked on Macon's door and he called us in immediately. Apparently, we had come just in the nick of time because Mother looked ready to murder Macon.

"Marin, I'm glad you're here," Macon said as he eyed the Elf Queen with fear.

"Please tell me you did not agree to be used as bait?!" she asked with flames dancing within her eyes.

"Of course, I did," I said honestly. "It's the best way to discover who is after me."

"Are you mad?" she asked me. "You could be killed!"

"I could be killed as a Mercenary, yet you allow me to complete this training to follow that path. Why is this different?"

"Because someone is after you with the intent of kidnapping you, which will possibly lead to your death," Father said matter-of-factly.

"There is no other way for us to discovery who it is. Besides, if they wanted to kill me, they could have just ordered the bandits who attacked us to do it," I replied in a neutral tone so as not to upset him.

"I told you she wouldn't listen to reason," Favian said to Father.

"What are you planning for this *test*?" Mother asked as she sat down in the chair beside Father.

Macon relaxed now that she had sat down and said, "We are going to have Favian and Marin go to the town square and appear as though they are shopping for gifts to try to lure the kidnappers out. The rest of the sixth years will be spread throughout the town either in hiding spots or shopping as well with some at each escape point in case something goes wrong.

Masters Sean and Martin, as well as myself, will be watching as well. She will be completely protected."

"I don't like it," Mother said and shook her head.

Father put his hand on Mother's and smiled. "Dear, it is a good plan."

"They are going to risk her life!" Mother said. "That is never a good plan."

"You cannot protect me all the time," I told her.

"You cannot risk your life all the time," she said back to me. "Are you telling me that I cannot become a Mercenary?" I asked her softly. She turned her head away and my anger skyrocketed. "It is my life and I will decide what to do with it. I am going to be a Mercenary. I am going to go through with this test. There is nothing you can do to stop me. If you take me back to the castle I will escape and come back. If you try to hold me against my will, I will attack any who guard me and escape. I will do as I wish," I said angrily before storming out of Macon's office and walking to the stables.

Fire nickered in greeting to me and I hurried to her stall, burying my face against her neck as I cried. I had training in thirty minutes, but I was in no condition to practice my swordsmanship so I walked to the tack area and grabbed Fire's saddle and bridle, quickly tacking her and led her from the barn. I swung up onto her back and kissed to her. She took off at a fast gallop, eating the ground up quickly with her hooves as we passed the outdoor training arena and began the five-mile trip to my favorite hiding spot. Fire galloped happily since she hadn't been out of the stable and had been craving to stretch her legs.

She slowed as she started the climb up the side of the mountain and she was forced to use some of her energy for the steep climb. We rounded the mountain and I spotted the trail off to the right, slowing Fire so we could make the turn onto the mostly unused path. Most didn't know the trail existed or where it led, but during my first year I'd found it and had often visited it while attending the Academy. Fire was forced to walk since the path was narrow, steep and windy, but she didn't seem to mind. It took twenty minutes before we finally made it to a spot where the trees stopped fifteen feet away from a rock which overlooked the lake further down. I dismounted, dropped the reins on the ground, to ground-tie Fire, and then sat on the rock.

How could she do this to me? How could she plan to keep me from being a Mercenary? Why even let me go to the Academy if she wasn't going to let me do the job afterwards? I felt awful for the way I had spoken to her, but I had meant every word. I greatly appreciated them raising me as if I were one of their own, but she couldn't force me to stay at the castle. I wasn't built to be a lady who sat on her hands and let the men go off and fight. I was a fighter and I needed to be out slaying ogres and protecting defenseless people.

Tears leaked from my eyes again and I hated that I was crying yet *again*! I rolled onto my back and let the tears flow as the sun warmed my face and body. Before I'd realized it, I had fallen asleep and then was woken by Fire's nicker. "How did you find me?" I asked Favian without sitting up or opening my eyes. I knew it was Ice who'd come, by the way

Fire had nickered so I didn't need to look to know it was Favian on his back.

"I followed you here when we were second years after you had that fight with Brock and he'd upset you," Favian said as he sat down beside me.

"Have you come to take me to Mother so that she can lock me up in the castle's dungeon?" I asked.

"No," Favian said with a laugh. "Though I have thought of doing that a few times."

"Everything I said was the truth," I told him softly. "She cannot keep me from being who I really am. I am not a lady to stay at the castle while you go off and fight battles."

"I know," he said. "And she knows that as well. She is simply worried for your safety as I was."

"Is that why you got so mad? Because you are worried for me? Or was it because I'm your partner and wouldn't listen to you?" I asked as I opened my eyes to look at him.

He nodded. "All of that. You are very stubborn," he said with a smile.

"As if you aren't," I teased.

He laughed and then went silent and still. I saw his face change from happy to serious as he listened to something in the distance. The tree leaves rustled in the wind and Favian's silver hair swayed with the breeze. I wanted to run my fingers through it to see if it was as soft as it looked, but I kept my hands where they were. The horses were also turning their ears in search of whatever they were hearing. I wanted to ask what it was, but he would just shush me so I waited for him to tell me.

My patience was growing thin when Favian suddenly jumped on top of me, shielding my body with his. I heard the sound of arrows striking the ground near us and tried to throw him off of me so that he could protect himself. Arrows whizzed past our bodies and their metal heads buried into the ground just past our feet. There had to be at least four shooters to release that many arrows at once. "Favian get off of me! Run to the trees!" I told him. If we didn't move soon the shooters would correct their aim and then his back would look like a porcupine's.

He stared down into my eyes and shook his head. "You won't make it to the trees without getting hit."

"You're going to get hit if you don't get off of me. Now get off and we'll run."

The arrows slowed and Favian's jaw clenched. "You run as fast as you can. Understand?" As if I needed to be told that!

I nodded and he jumped off of me and grabbed my hand, pulling me to my feet and we started running. The arrows increased in number and this time they were aimed directly at us and I could see they were coming from the road. Favian and I dodged the arrows right and left as we ran for cover, the sound of them whizzing past our ears like angry wasps. We made it to the trees and I pressed my body against the trunk of a tree, folding my arms against the front of my body so they wouldn't get hit by arrows.

"Who is it?" I asked. "Is this a test?"

"I don't know," Favian said angrily. "They aren't talking and I can't see them through the woods."

Fire neighed from off to my right and I turned to

find her looking around for me. She spotted me and screamed a horse scream of fear and worry and then started to run towards me. I yelled at her to stop, but she didn't listen. She ran to me and I did the only thing I could do, I grabbed onto her saddle and let her take me away from Favian and the arrows. I didn't want to leave him, but if I had let Fire stand near me, she would have been hit by the arrows. I couldn't let her get injured because of me.

Favian whistled and I heard Ice whinny in response and knew he would be after me soon. Fire took a side path which was dangerously steep and led down to the lake. Unfortunately, it was the only path besides the one we'd taken to get there and despite its dangerousness it was the only way for us to get out alive. Fire grunted with effort as she made her way down the path, trying to keep me alive. I could hear Favian and Ice behind us, but didn't dare turn around for fear or throwing Fire off balance. We were almost to the bottom when arrows began flying over our heads. Fire blew loudly out of her nose in frustration and then finally jumped down the last five feet to the flat wide trail around the lake. Her muscles bunched as she prepared to gallop around the trail, but I pulled on her reins, making her wait for Favian and Ice. They finally made it down and Favian yelled, "What are you waiting for? Run!"

I loosened Fire's reins and she took off at a full gallop, turning right so that we were protected by the mountain from the arrows and our attackers. "How are we going to get back? They're on the only road that leads to the school?" I asked Favian as the horses carried us farther from our attackers.

"There is another path we can take," he said. "But I don't know if they'll have that blocked as well."

"It's our only choice," I told him. "We don't have any real weapons except our throwing knives." I desperately wished for my sword underneath my bed. "How did they get inside the grounds?" This was not a test; Macon wouldn't allow us to be put in so much danger. How had they gotten passed everyone without being noticed? Had they slipped in the back way and gone unseen by the guard there?

"I don't know," Favian said angrily. "But we need to find out." We slowed the horses since we were out of immediate danger and didn't want to use up all of their energy yet. "Follow me," Favian said as he steered Ice off of the path and into the trees> "And watch your back," he reminded me.

I followed him silently, listening for any sound out of place or any sight to indicate that we might be walking into a trap. We had been through several tests similar to this, but this was the first real problem we had experienced. This was the first time our lives were on the line. Surprisingly, I felt very calm and not even a little bit scared as we made our way through the forest as silently as we could.

Favian stopped Ice and Fire stopped behind him. I heard the noise too, which meant it was close so I went on high alert, looking everywhere for a potential threat. Unfortunately, we weren't prepared for the attackers to be right above us, having been camouflaged so well that the horses and Favian didn't pick up their scents or bodies.

Two attackers dropped down from the trees onto Favian, pulling him from Ice's saddle, but Favian saw them move just before they dropped and had pulled his knives to fight them. Both attackers had dark masks on so I couldn't see what type of being they were or who they were.

I didn't have long to watch because another attacker dropped from the tree above me and landed on Fire's back right behind me. I tried to turn to fight my attacker, but they wrapped their arms around my waist, grabbed the reins and dug their heels into Fire, making her spin around and run in the opposite direction.

I slowly reached down and grabbed the top of my throwing knife and stabbed the person in their arm, making them cry out in pain. "Whoa!" I yelled to Fire who instantly stopped and made my attacker slam their face into the back of my head. I stabbed their leg with my other knife and then swung my right leg up and around in a dismounting move that also knocked them from Fire's back. It was a technique Kato had taught me and the trick almost worked. I would have stayed in Fire's saddle, but they grabbed my left leg and jerked it out of the stirrup, throwing me off balance and pulling me off of her. Fire moved around me and started stomping her hooves, trying to kill my attacker as I stood up and prepared to attack.

I clucked to Fire to tell her to back off and pinned my attacker to the ground and stabbed my blade through their shoulder. "Who are you?" I asked angrily.

"Screw you," they said venomously.

I ripped the mask off and stared at the human

man's face. I had no idea who he was. "Who sent you?" I asked.

"I came on my own," he said as he tried to buck me off of his body. I stabbed him in the stomach and twisted the knife as hard as I could, making him scream out in pain. "You can kill me, but more will come," he growled.

"Why do you want me dead?" I asked.

"He doesn't want you dead," he said. "He wants to see you in person."

"Who! Who is 'he'!" I screamed and then put the knife against the man's throat.

"You'll find out soon enough," he said with a sneer.

I didn't have time to tie him up for questioning later and I needed to check on Favian so I slit his throat and hopped back up onto Fire's back, squeezing my legs and kissing to her to make her run back to Favian and Ice. We arrived to find Favian pinning a Goblin to the ground and questioning him.

"I'm alive," I told Favian as I dismounted Fire and walked up to him. The other attacker was dead and another human.

"More will come. They will come until she is taken to him," The goblin said.

"Who is he?" I asked. "What does he want with me?"

"You'll meet him soon enough," the Goblin said. "And we only know the reason we don't want you here."

"Why don't you want her here?" Favian asked. "What has she done to deserve your hatred?"

"She is here," the goblin said. "That is why."

"That doesn't make any sense," I said angrily. "What does me being alive have to do with anything?"

"If he does not rectify the problem, someone else will," the goblin said. "You cannot be allowed to finish."

"Finish?" Favian asked. "Finish what? The Academy?"

The Goblin bucked his body upwards as he tried to reach for a knife, but Favian stabbed his knife into the Goblin's throat before he could finish the movement, killing him. "We have to go," I said seriously. "There might be more." Favian cleaned his knives on the Goblin's shirt and put them away before he hopped up onto Ice. I remounted Fire and made sure my daggers were in place. "How did they get in here?" I asked him angrily.

He pointed to the brand on the human's right arm, the brand one received once they completed the Academy. "They attended here when they were younger," he said.

"So other Mercenaries and guards are after me?" I asked in shock, now starting to feel fear.

"It seems so," Favian said. We walked the horses in silence a moment as he thought and then he said, "We need to get to Macon quickly."

I nodded and we asked the horses to trot, weaving through the trees and looking for potential threats. I didn't understand why Mercenaries would be after me. I hadn't done anything on my missions that could have upset anyone. Favian and I had only done three missions so far. The first was a simple guard mission where we had protected a young Prince as he traveled from one city to the next and we didn't even encounter any problems then. Our second mission had been to thwart a group of bandits that had been terrorizing a small farming village and we'd only killed three of the bandits before the other six ran off, never to be heard from again. I had gotten a severe cut on my leg and had had to be rushed to a healer before I bled out, but nothing else had gone wrong. The third mission was to track down and kill three rogue ogres which had started eating humans. That was our most difficult mission and one that had almost killed Favian as he had tried to protect me and not paid attention to his back.

All of those had gone well in Mercenary standards, so I didn't understand how I could have gotten enemies if I'd done everything right.

We finally made it back to the main grounds to find the students in chaos. As we approached Master Sean ran to us. "Favian! Marin! Are you both alright?"

I nodded. "Yes, sir."

"Cesar heard Fire scream and we tried to find you two, but we didn't know where you had gone."

"We were attacked by archers initially, but managed to get away from them only to run into a trap with three others," Favian said. "We must speak to Macon immediately."

Master Sean nodded and held his hands out for our horse's reins. "Go, I'll tend to your mounts."

We dismounted and ran to the building to find Father and Mother arguing with Master Martin and

Macon. "Father!" I yelled.

Father and Mother turned and then something hard hit the back of my head. I tried to see who had hit me, but the hit was perfectly executed and it knocked me unconscious.

6

"Let me out!" I yelled angrily from where I was chained to a stone wall in the darkest dungeon cell in the Elven Kingdom.

I'd woken up an hour earlier to find myself chained and alone in the dungeon. Having played here a lot as a child, it hadn't taken me long to figure out where I was. The dirt beneath me was cool and clean and the chains on my wrists and ankles were warm against my skin. I didn't know how they had gotten me from the Academy to the dungeon without me waking up, but no matter how it was done, I was thoroughly pissed off.

"I demand that you let me out!" I yelled again. I jerked against the chains, hoping they might be old and the bolts would be loose, but no such luck. These chains were enchanted and I had no chance of breaking them. Luckily there weren't any rats at the moment to pester me.

I looked around the cell and spotted the bucket

that I was to use as a restroom and sighed loudly. "Couldn't you have at least given me a bigger bucket?" I asked no one.

The chains were long enough that I could walk around, but since I couldn't walk out of the cell, I simply used the bucket and then sat back down against the wall. It wasn't embarrassing like some would have thought since I had been in worse situations and had had to use worse areas as restrooms.

A reflection of light appeared against the outside of the cell, which meant that someone was coming with a torch in my direction. I listened for footsteps, but of course the Elves had silent footsteps and I couldn't hear anything.

"Are you done yelling?" Kato asked from the doorway.

"No!" I screamed at him. "Not you too! Please, Kato. Let me out of here. How can you let them torture me so?"

"They are protecting you, Marin. You would see that if you weren't so busy being angry that they knocked you out and brought you here," he said as he opened my cell and stepped inside. One of the maids was with him, holding the torch while Kato held a long silver tray which had food and drink on it.

"Is this my last meal?" I asked crossly.

"Calm your anger. It's not becoming of a lady," Mother said as she stepped inside the cell behind Kato.

I stood up and jerked at the end of the length of the chains. "I'm not a lady!" I screamed at her. "I'm a fighter! I'm a Mercenary!"

"You are in no shape to yell at me," she said with a

straight face. "I'm sorry that you are upset, but yelling will not change your current situation."

"What will?" I asked her.

"You agreeing to drop out of the Academy and not pursue the life of a Mercenary," she said straight-faced.

"No," I told her adamantly. "Never."

"You have proven that females can attend the Academy as well. You have proven that women can be Mercenaries. You have proven your point," she said angrily.

"I never wanted to prove a point. That is not the reason I joined at all," I told her honestly. "I only wanted to live my life. I am not a lady. I am not made to wear dresses and prance around the castle. I am made to fight and kill and maim. I am a killer," I told her. "And chaining me up down here won't change that. Nothing you do will change that."

"You choose your life," she said. "You can choose to be a lady if you want." She had an incredibly sad look on her face and I felt awful, but I would not back down from this.

"Why do you want me to be something that I'm not?" I asked her painfully. "I thought you loved me for who I am?"

A single tear slipped down her cheek and she said, "I love you for who you are, but who you are is getting you attacked. I will not let you continue to put your life in jeopardy."

"Listen to her, Marin. She is only looking out for your wellbeing," Kato said.

I glared at him. "If she told you that you couldn't

be a guard anymore, that you had to sit around the castle and do nothing, would you?"

"I would," he said honestly.

I rolled my eyes. "Not if she ordered you to, but if she asked you to."

Kato smiled. "I have been alive a lot longer than you. You are not going to catch me in a question like this."

"Please, Mother. If you do love me then let me out."

"No, not until you understand," she said angrily. "Leave her the food and let us make our exit," she ordered in her Queenly tone.

Kato handed me the tray of food and I let it drop upside down on the ground. "If you will not let me go, then I will not eat," I said as I sat down against the wall and crossed my arms over my chest.

"You must eat," Kato said.

"You must let me go."

"Leave her be, Kato. She will change her mind in a couple of days when the hunger is gnawing at her innards," Mother said as she turned away.

They left me and my stupid female emotions took over, making me cry again. I sobbed loudly as I sat, chained in the underground of my home. How was it possible to have so many tears in one's body?

I couldn't believe that she was actually keeping me prisoner. My heart was twisted with a mixture of anger and sadness that left me feeling completely betrayed.

I waited until I heard them shut the door at the other end of the tunnel which led out of the cells and up to the castle. I waited a moment longer to be sure and then stood up. A benefit to playing in these cells was being able to hide things here and find escapes while no one was watching me. I crawled along the wall, running my hands along the stones in search of a particular one that wasn't actually secured. A rat squeaked in protest when I got too close to it and I hit it with the back of my head, pushing it away. I did not feel like getting bitten today.

I finally felt a stone move and smiled. Bingo. I started to tug on the stone, but then I heard the door open to the dungeon and crawled back to the center of my chains and sat with my head bowed trying to look miserable. It wasn't very hard to do.

My cell door opened and a torch was placed in the holder near me. "Refusing to eat?" Favian asked. It pained me that he was here and not unchaining me even more than Mother's visit had pained me.

"I refuse to live as a lady. I will only live if I'm allowed to be what I am, not something she wants me to be."

He sat down cross-legged in front of me and said, "That's not the true reason why you're down here, you know. That's just her side agenda. The real reason you're down here is to protect you from the people trying to kidnap you. We are using all of our resources to locate the ring leader while you are safe in Elven territory."

"Then why am I chained?" I asked bitterly as I showed him my wrists.

"Because we know you'll just run back to the Academy to complete the training if we don't keep you chained up."

"You're going to go back, aren't you?" He didn't respond, which was answer enough. "So, you're going to go back, complete the program and become a Mercenary while I'm held prisoner. Then when I am finally let out, I'll not be able to complete the program and have no job and no partner."

"We're still partners, Marin," he said seriously.

I looked up and met his eyes. "If we were still partners you would help me out of my captivity."

"You haven't been kidnapped. You've been grounded," he said. "And it is well within a parent's right to ground their child."

"You wouldn't allow this for yourself!" I yelled at him. "You would demand that I let you free and be furious with me if I didn't."

"I know," he said with a sigh. "But I cannot free you. I have to ensure that you're safe and protected and this is the best way."

He stood up and I whispered, "Don't do this, Favian."

"I'm sorry," he whispered and grabbed the torch from the wall. "Favian! Don't do this to me! Don't abandon me!" I cried.

He set the torch back and squatted down in front of me, holding my face between his hands. "I am not abandoning you. I am protecting you! You'll understand sooner or later. I must protect you." He put something bitter inside my mouth and held my face with his hands, forcing me to swallow. "If you won't eat, I'll force nourishment down your throat. Sleep, Marin and be safe. All I ask is that you're safe." He kissed my forehead, grabbed the torch, and left, closing the cell door behind him.

I tried to gag up what he had given me, but it was futile. "Favian!" I yelled. "Favian don't leave me!"

No matter how much I cried, he did not respond. He had left me alone. My partner had abandoned me. I cried until the medicine he had given me took effect and then fell into a drugged sleep, dreaming of those that had betrayed me.

"Rise and shine," Kato said as he set a new tray of food on the ground in front of me. "Time to eat."

"I'm not eating," I mumbled as I sat up groggily. I looked up at the window and stared at the darkness outside. "Is it the same night or the second?"

"The third actually," Kato said. "Favian wanted to ensure you got plenty of rest. Now, eat up." He pushed the tray of food towards me and I flung it to the side with my hand, sending it end over end and spreading the food throughout the cell.

"I'm not eating. And you tell Favian to stay away from me or he won't like our next encounter," I said cruelly.

"Do not be so hard on your friend. He only cares for your safety as do the rest of us."

"None of you care for me. If you cared, you would let me out of these chains and free me."

"What if it was Favian in your place? What if someone was trying to kill him and he wanted to go confront them? What would you do?"

"I would go with him and watch his back," I said immediately without any thought. "I would not put him in a dark, dungeon cell."

Kato shook his head sadly. "You better eat what food you can salvage or you and Favian will have that confrontation. And I know you don't really want to fight him."

I watched him leave and then listened for the door at the end to close. I had to get out. I had to get out now before Favian drugged me again.

I crawled back down the wall and found the stone again, this time quicker since I remembered approximately how far down I had gone. It would have been much easier if I could have woken up during the day and had sunlight, but life was rarely easy. I tugged on the stone, back and forth, back and forth until it finally came completely out of the wall. I reached inside slowly, running my fingertips along the floor until they hit a small piece of cold metal. I pulled it out and quickly unlocked my chains with the key. I stood up and stretched, letting my small freedom relax me.

Now came the difficult part. There was a small window, fourteen feet above the ground, but it was nearly impossible to reach unless you had someone else's shoulders to stand on and even then, you had to jump up from their shoulders to the ledge of the window and pull yourself up. Then you had to break the window and pull yourself out without getting cut on the glass. Fortunately, I had broken the glass on accident when I was a toddler when I had thrown a ball this direction while Favian and I were playing outside. Later I had come down here and cleared out all of the glass and had used this as a quick escape when Favian and I were playing tag. I searched along the wall for the rope I'd tied to the outside to crawl out, but of course they had removed it before putting me inside.

I cursed angrily and searched around for something useful within the cell. I came up with nothing as I had expected. Favian had probably come down here himself and searched everything and taken out the rope to ensure that I couldn't escape. I was very glad I had hidden the key without him knowing and very glad I had never told him about it. I grabbed a rock and threw it across the cell as hard as I could, hitting the cell door in my anger. I heard yelling outside and stopped moving, afraid someone had heard me throw the rock.

"Get your swords and shields!" Kato yelled. "The boundary is being attacked."

Attacked? Who would attack the Elves?

"Squad one to the eastern section. Squad two to the western. Squad three with me."

"Who's attacking us?" I heard Favian ask. "Ogres. Hundreds of them," Kato answered.

My blood boiled and I almost yelled to Favian to get me out, but I bit my tongue. I hated ogres more than anything else in the world. It was my goal in life to kill them all. I didn't care that they were technically a species like humans and Elves. They may have started off good, but over the past fifty years they had turned evil and needed to die. I waited until I heard them all move away from the window and then backed up ten paces, which put my back against the cell door. I didn't think I could make it, but I had to. I had to get out. I had to fight. I took a deep breath to calm myself and then ran forward as fast as I could. I waited until the last second and then jumped up as high as I could jump, higher than ever before. I reached with my fingers and somehow managed to grab the window ledge.

I'd made it! I held in my scream of victory, so that I wouldn't alert them to my presence, pulled myself up slowly and then peered out into the night. The window was at ground level so I couldn't see very much except grass and bushes, but it seemed clear and I couldn't hear anyone nearby. I reached forward and pulled myself up and into the window and then out of the hole. Thank goodness I was still thin or I would have never been able to fit through the window. I stayed lying down as I looked around, waiting for any change. Nothing. I jumped up and ran to the right, hugging the wall of the castle as I neared the armory. There were a couple of voices, but it sounded like it was only the blacksmith's assistants. They were big boys, but they were slow and I could grab swords and run back out before they could catch me. Of course, they would immediately alert everyone to my escape, but I had to hope that I could make it out of the main gate to fight the ogres before they found me.

Fire burned within me, urging me on to complete this mission. Where had this come from? Why did I feel so energized? I waited until the blacksmith's assistants' backs were turned and then ran into the armory, grabbed two swords and ran out.

"Wait!" They called.

"Stop! You're not supposed to fight!"

I ignored them and made a mad dash for the front gate. I ran by Kato just as the blacksmith's assistants yelled, "Marin's escaped!"

I continued out of the gates, ignoring the shocked shouts of the guards and then ran into the barrier. The barrier pressed against me, trying to hold me inside its boundaries. I growled in frustration and pushed against it as I heard Kato and the guards closing in on me. I couldn't let them catch me. I had to kill the ogres! I screamed in anger and tore through the barrier, running out onto the open road and stopped as I came within sight of the ogres.

They were grotesque, fat, sloppy looking beasts with mildew green skin, dirt brown eyes and stood over fifteen feet tall. They were completely hairless and wore loincloths to cover their genitals. They bared their teeth at me, showing the few that remained and I could smell their foul stench from one hundred yards away. "Leave this place or die!" I yelled as my fury ignited and a fire

I hadn't known lived within me spread throughout my body. "We've come to take you," one of the ogres said. "Come peace-

fully and we will not slaughter the Elves."

"The only ones about to be slaughtered are you!" I screamed as I charged forward. The ogres screamed back at me and the stench of their breath stole my breath away for a moment before I plowed on and started hacking at them. Ogres were the only beasts that made me lose control. They had killed my family when I was a toddler. They killed innocent people and

111

ate their bones. They were murderous beasts and I had taken it upon myself to make it my job to kill them. As I hacked off arms and heads, my blood boiled and a smile split my face. This was when I was truly happy. This was the time I relished.

The ogres swarmed around me, but the only thing they gained by their closeness to me was their death. Ogre bodies piled up around me and their blood coated my swords and splashed along my arms, chest and face. I finished off the twenty that had been in front of the main gate and ran to the right, towards the battle raging on the eastern side.

"Marin!" Cesar yelled at me. "Return to the castle at once."

I ignored his call. I only had one thing to do. Kill the ogres. A group of Elf soldiers stood between me and the ogres. They didn't see me because they were preparing to confront the ogres in the other direction so I jumped up and did a front flip over the top of the soldiers, landing on my feet in front of them. Some of the soldiers gasped in shock while others backed away. I sprinted forward and attacked the ogres before me, ignoring the Elves.

The sight of them falling before my blade was intoxicating and I wanted more. I needed more ogres' deaths! With a swiftness I had not known I possessed until then, I slew the fifty ogres on the eastern side in only a couple of minutes and then ran on to reach the southern side. I rounded the corner and saw Favian standing amongst the ogres, killing again and again, but there were at least one hundred and fifty ogres and he was greatly outnumbered. I smiled wide and ran into the swarm of beasts, slicing and hacking and killing.

I heard Favian talking to me, but I ignored him. I would not be denied this chance. I would not be denied this opportunity to rid the world of so many ogres at once. I slew the last ogre and dashed away before Favian could grab me from behind. I could hear the Elves behind me, following me, but they didn't matter. I reached the western side and was saddened to see only ten ogres left alive, Kato's blade having finished off the rest.

I ran forward and pushed Kato aside so that I could finish the last of them. I killed nine of them quickly and then faced off with the last one. He met my eyes and growled. "You were supposed to come alive. You have killed too many of mine to be allowed to live now though," he said angrily.

"I will kill you all before I cease to exist on this planet," I told him. "I will rid the world of your putrid existence."

"If you think you are so tough then come at me, little girl. Let me see what you can do with those blades."

"Marin, stop," Favian said from behind me. "You need to calm down."

"Please, Marin, listen to him," Father said.

"I do not listen to those who stand in the way of my path, even if I love any of them. I do not listen to those who would hold me back from my destiny," I growled as I spun around to face them. I felt abnormal. I felt taller and faster and better than ever before. I felt amazing, but the words that came out of my mouth were foreign and yet seemed right. Where was all of this coming from?

"What is your destiny?" Father asked.

I smiled. "You already know, don't you King of the Elves?" Father looked at me in bewilderment and then I heard the ogre move behind me. I spun around in a perfect three-hundred-and-sixty-degree turn, my arms out and my swords raised, slicing his head off and sending it flying through the air. The ogre's body fell and I smiled. I felt a slight disappointment and said, "I have killed them all. I only wish there had been more." I turned around and confirmed that there were no ogres left alive and then my body's energy disappeared and I fainted.

7

I woke up in the healer's quarters, strapped to the bed. I sighed loudly. "Must we continue to tie me to things?" I asked as I looked around for anyone.

Father and Favian walked inside the room and stood facing me with matching worried looks on their faces. "How do you feel?" Favian asked.

"I feel irritated. How come the barrier kept me from leaving the Elven Kingdom?" I asked. "Why did I pass out when I hit it?"

"That's the last thing you remember?" Father asked. "You remember running into the barrier and then nothing else?"

I nodded. "Yes. Why? Did I do something embarrassing?" I looked at Favian who looked paler than usual.

The healer, a kind old female Elf named Lila with white hair which was always in a single long braid that hung down her back walked inside the room. "How are you feeling?" she asked me with a smile.

"Hungry and frustrated," I replied.

Father whispered something into the Lila's ear and her eyes widened in shock. "She remembers nothing after that?"

Father and Favian shook their heads. "What's going on?" I asked. "Why are you all acting like I did something crazy?"

Favian sat down on the edge of my bed and said, "You didn't pass out from the barrier Marin. You broke through it and fought the ogres."

"I did?" I asked in shock. "Well, did I win? I don't feel any cuts of bruises."

"Yes, you won," he said with a smirk. "Actually, you defeated them all by yourself. You defeated over two hundred ogres by yourself."

I stared at him in disbelief and shock. "Why don't I remember it?" This was frightening to me. What if I had gone crazy and attacked the Elves? What if I had hurt Favian in my trance?

Father shook his head. "I'm not sure. You talked to us as well, but you were not yourself."

"What did I say?" I asked.

"That's enough. She must have suffered some type of memory loss and we don't want to push her too far," Lila said sternly.

"Why don't I remember?" I asked myself. "Why can't I remember what happened?"

"Lila, undo her bonds," Father said.

"Father!" Favian said in shock. "You can't let her go. She'll return to the Academy."

Father nodded. "Yes, she will and that is exactly what she needs to do. It is clear that no matter what we try, she will escape. Besides, it is clear that she has a destiny to complete."

Favian's jaw tightened. "She could be kidnapped or killed." Father put his hand on his son's shoulder. "Then you had better return with her to protect her." He stared deep into Favian's eyes and said, "We must not keep her from her destiny."

Favian glanced at me and then sighed. "I understand."

"I don't!" I yelled. "Why are you acting like you know of some destiny I have when I do not!"

"We don't *know* your destiny, but we know you have one," Favian said. "He's right that we can't keep someone from completing it. If we did, you would end up resenting us." He gripped my arm. "And I could not live with myself if you hated me."

"Stay here for the night so that we can be sure you're alright and then tomorrow morning you can both head back to the Academy. Deal?" Father asked.

My head was swirling with all of this craziness. First the Elves kidnap me and lock me in a dungeon and then I kill over two hundred ogres by myself and cannot remember a single event. I nodded to Father and stood up as soon as Lila unstrapped me. I hugged Favian and then Father. "I know you were trying to protect me, but you cannot keep me locked in a dungeon. Thank you for understanding."

"You're welcome. And go easy on your mother. She only wants what is best for you."

I smiled. "I know."

I followed behind Favian and Father out of the

healer's room and down the hall. I was about to follow Father to the dining hall, but Favian pulled me to the side and stared at me. "Are we okay?" he asked.

"Are you going to lock me up in the dungeon again?" I asked. He sighed. "No, but you must understand why I did it?"

I nodded and hugged him. "Thank you for caring so much about me. I was very mad when I was down there, but whatever happened during that battle has really calmed me and allowed me to see things more clearly." Though I wished desperately to remember that battle. How had I killed two hundred ogres by myself? How was that possible?

"You truly frightened me," he whispered as he hugged me back. "I did not like seeing you that way. It wasn't you."

"Now you know how I felt during our battle in my trial." He sighed. "Let's promise not to fight again, okay?"

I pulled back from our hug, held out my hand and he shook it. "Deal," I said with a smile.

"Marin!" Mother yelled as she ran down the hallway with her dress in her hands so she wouldn't trip over it. She looked like she was floating and her face looked as angelic as ever. How I envied her beauty. She wrapped me up in a hug and immediately started crying. "I'm so sorry. Please forgive me. Please don't be mad at me."

I hugged her and patted her back reassuringly. "I'm not mad at you, Mother. I forgive you."

She pulled back and then gave me the mother glare. "Don't you ever run out onto the battlefield without Favian beside you again! Do you understand me?!"

I giggled and nodded. "I promise." She smiled. "Good, now let's go eat dinner."

"You didn't happen to grab some meat for me, did you? I'm starving," I said as we walked and I rubbed my growling stomach. "No, but we can pick some up on the way to school," Favian said. "I saw you eyeing the shop on the way in last week."

"I try not to complain when I'm here and most of the time I'm fine, but I am really craving meat right now," I said as we headed into the dining hall.

"No more talk about that," Mother chastised me. "Now you must act like a lady." She looked at my dirty pants and shirt and said, "Since you cannot look like one at the moment."

We stepped into the hall with Favian and me giggling to be bombarded by Amile as she shoved me out of the way to fawn over Favian. "Are you alright? I heard you battled the ogres yesterday. Were you injured?" she asked.

My fists clenched at my sides and I was ready to punch her when Father put his arm around my shoulders and steered me away from them. "You look thirsty, are you thirsty?"

"I'm irritated," I said. "Though, I'm not sure why."

He laughed. "I'm sure you will figure it out soon. You are a very smart girl."

Favian detached himself from Amile's claws and took his seat next to mine. "The chef went all out!" he said happily as he surveyed the banquet on the table.

I looked at the new bracelet on his wrist and bit

my lip. I did not want to make a scene like I'd done last time. Besides, why should I care if he received gifts from his subjects? Weren't the royals supposed to be given gifts? At least he was still wearing my necklace.

"Yes, it seems so," I replied.

We ate our food and talked about anything not dealing with the Academy or the ogre attack and I actually enjoyed myself quite a bit. I truly had forgiven everyone for the hostage situation and knew they had only done it out of love, despite my mood initially. It was strange how feelings could change so quickly.

I had just finished my food when Maddock, a close friend of mine and Favian's and a very handsome Elf, said my name softly to get my attention. He was one of the few Elves with blonde hair instead of silver and also one of the few with arm muscles.

I stood up and curtsied to him, playing the lady as Mother would have wanted me to. "Maddock, what brings you to my side?" I asked with a smile.

"Would you take a walk with me?" he asked. "I'd like to speak with you."

I looked at Mother who nodded happily.

"Of course," I said.

"It's not safe for her to be alone," Favian said as he stood up with an irritated look on his face.

"She is not alone," Mother said. "Maddock is with her. I'm sure he would protect her if need be?"

Maddock bowed. "Of course, Queen Amadis."

She nodded again. "Then please be on your way."

"Mother," Favian began.

She shushed him. "Sit down and finish your food."

Maddock extended his bent elbow to me and I set

my hand on it, letting him lead me from the dining hall. "I'm very happy to see that you are well," he said as we walked down the hallway. "I heard you fought very hard yesterday."

"That's what I hear as well," I said with a smile. He opened the back door and we walked out into Mother's rose garden. "What has brought your urgent attention to me this night?" I asked him. It wasn't rare for him to visit me to go on rides or spar, but he had never visited me like this before.

He stopped at the stone bench in the center and we sat down on it. The roses were in full bloom all year long thanks to Mother's magic and the reds and yellows were bright even in the darkness. "I came to be sure you were alright and to speak to you before you left for the Academy again," he said.

"Thank you for your concern. I am feeling very well."

He turned to face me and said, "I wanted to give you a token of my friendship." He pulled out a shell necklace and set it in my hands. "I know you aren't technically royalty, but I hope that you will still accept this as my friend. I worry for your safety and hope that maybe this will assist you someday in the future."

"It's very beautiful," I said sincerely.

"If you whisper the Elven word for fire, it will light anything touching it on fire, except you of course."

I stared at the shell necklace in disbelief. "Really?" He nodded. "Yes, I'll show you."

He put the necklace on his own neck and then picked up a yellow flower petal from the ground, wrapping it around the necklace. "Fira."

The petal burst into flame and drifted away from him to settle on the ground in a charred little piece. He took the necklace off and I was shocked to see no burn marks on his throat. "That is truly amazing," I said in astonishment.

He smiled. "So, you'll accept it?"

I smiled. "I would have accepted it if it had been a simple shell necklace, Maddock. You have been a good friend to me and I truly appreciate it. Not everyone would take to a human living amongst the Elves."

He tied the necklace around my neck and shook his head. "I would fight each and every one of them if I could."

I laughed at the inside joke. We had all been fighting various Elves over that issue for as long as I could remember. "Remember when I fought the older girl and she ran to Amadis crying about her muddy dress only to have Amadis punish her for being cruel to me?" I asked him.

Maddock laughed. "Yes, that was very entertaining watching you knock her into the mud puddle and then throw mud on her face."

"I'm sorry I am gone so long at school, but soon it'll be over."

He shrugged. "And then you and Favian will be out on missions as Mercenaries."

"I'll visit often," I promised him and then punched his arm playfully. "Who else will be here to put you in your proper place?"

He laughed and then hugged me quickly. "You are a good person, Marin. Don't ever forget that."

I wasn't sure why he had said that, but I smiled

back at him and then stood up. "I should get to bed and ensure everything is packed for the trip tomorrow. Thank you again for the necklace."

He bowed to me and then kissed the back of my hand formerly. "Good night, Princess Marin."

I frowned at him. "I am not the princess. Stop that."

He smiled. "In my eyes, you've always been a princess." With my face stuck on dumb, he left the garden and left me to stand in utter disbelief. Had he just flirted with me? Surely, I had misinterpreted that. Surely, he only meant it because I was raised with Favian in the castle by the King and Queen, right? Right.

I walked into the castle and found Favian pacing up and down the hall. He spotted me and hurried over. "What happened? What did he want?" His eyes found the necklace and he asked, "Did he give you that? Did you accept it? Why are you wearing it?"

I ignored all of his questions, looked down at his wrist and said, "Amile must truly like you to have made a replacement piece so quickly for you." He looked at the bracelet and then sighed. I patted his shoulder. "You know Maddock and I are friends. You two are best friends, Favian. He gave me a gift to protect me, that's all."

"What does it do?" he asked curiously as he followed me down the hallway.

"If you are so curious, go ask him."

Favian turned me around and asked, "Did he ask to court you?"

I laughed so hard that I began crying as the

ridiculous notion was hilarious to me. "Favian, you are very comical. Of course not. He simply gave me a gift as a friend." I looked at his bracelet. "Wait, is that why she gave you that? Are you courting her?"

He glared at me. "No, I'm not courting her." He leaned forward and whispered, "Have you seen her face? She is homely."

I smiled. "Oh, so she's courting you?!" He glared harder at me. "No."

I shrugged and continued to smile at him. "Whatever. I don't care. Good night, Favian. I'll see you and the horses in the morning." I jogged up to my room and grabbed clothes to change into and then hurried to the bathing room.

The maid who worked in the bathing room was a female Elf about my age and she and I had been good friends, at least as good of friends as I could be with a female that I rarely saw. She smiled at me when I came in and said, "I knew you'd be coming for a bath. I could smell your stench from here."

I laughed. "If you knew, then you should have had my bath all ready," I teased back.

"You're too dirty for a bath as usual. To the stones with you," she ordered.

I stripped my dirty clothes off and tossed them onto the floor in the corner. She always washed my clothes for me and returned them to my bed afterwards. I walked down the tile floor to the stone area where she splashed warm water on me and then used a hard sponge to scrub at the ogre blood staining my body.

"One of these days I'd appreciate it if you came to me unstained," she muttered.

"If I weren't stained there would be no reason to come here."

She laughed. "Maybe you'd just like to smell nice for a certain boy."

I scoffed. "Boys smell just as dirty as me. Why should I clean myself when they don't?"

"Because ladies aren't supposed to smell like boys," she said in a very good imitation of Mother.

"Well, I'm not a lady."

She laughed loudly. "I'm well aware of that."

After scrubbing my body and hair clean, she poured a bucket of warm water over my head to rinse off the rest of the dirt and soap. I sighed happily. "That's my favorite part of this whole visit."

"Being clean?" she asked.

"Having the water dumped on my head."

She smiled. "I'll be sure to tell Prince Favian you like it. I'm sure he'd be more than willing to do it for you."

I gaped at her. "You wouldn't dare?" She shrugged. "Perhaps."

"You know if you told him that, he would dump water on me every chance he got."

She smiled. "I would love to watch it."

"You're cruel," I said mockingly.

"Go on to bed. You've got a long journey ahead of you. Plus, you'll be baked in dirt before you make it to school so all of my work is for naught."

"It makes me feel better so it's not for nothing," I assured her as I dried off and put my fresh clothes on.

"Be safe," she said to me as I walked out.

"You as well," I told her before jogging down

the hallway and up the stairs to my room. I crawled into my soft bed and warm covers and wished I could always have such niceties. That dungeon floor had not been comfortable.

Perhaps tomorrow I would complain to Favian about him not at least bringing me a pillow, while he'd held me prisoner. I closed my eyes and tried to remember what had happened the day before. It bothered me that I couldn't remember fighting all of the ogres. Had I been in some kind of trance? Or had something possessed my body? I would know if I was possessed, right?

If I had been possessed it would have made more sense for me to attack the Elves as opposed to the ogres though. So that ruled out possession. Unless, it was some part of me I always carried within, but that didn't make sense because I'd fought ogres before and never lost control of myself and forgotten what had happened.

It was all very suspect and I hoped to one day discover the truth of what had happened. Thinking on it would only upset me and keep me awake longer. I closed my eyes and willed myself to sleep, but I couldn't. I'd slept so much the past few days that I wasn't tired. I was just getting ready to sneak out of my room when someone knocked on it quietly.

I walked to the door and opened it, surprised to find Favian.

"What's up?" I asked him quietly so we wouldn't disturb anyone else.

He stepped into my room and shut the door behind him. "I can't sleep."

I smiled. "Me either, but at least I have an excuse, you drugged me so I slept a lot."

He frowned. "I thought you weren't mad anymore."

"I'm not mad. Stating a fact doesn't mean I'm mad. Why can't you sleep?"

He flopped down onto my bed and sighed. "I'm too worried."

I sat down next to him with my legs folded up underneath me. "Worried about what?"

He turned his head and looked at me, his grey eyes sparkling. "About you. I can't stop thinking about everything that has happened to you recently and about how we were attacked at the school."

"It'll all be alright," I assured him. "You don't know that."

I shrugged. "I have to believe it or you'll find me sitting in a corner rocking myself and screaming at shadows that move."

"What if I can't protect you?" he asked. "When I was fighting the Goblin and human in the forest, another one grabbed you and could have killed you."

"But he didn't because I protected myself," I said. "Favian, you can't be there to protect me all the time."

"Yes, I can," he said adamantly.

I lay down beside him and sighed. "It's not your job. I know you're noble and keep your word, but keeping a promise you made when you were four isn't the same. You didn't know back then what you were getting into and if you can't protect me, that's okay. I would never blame you if I got hurt and you hadn't

127

been able to prevent it."

"You're my best friend," he whispered as turned to face me. "I couldn't live with myself if…"

I put my hand over his mouth and whispered, "How do you think I feel? I feel exactly the same way, which is why I can't allow you to risk your life to protect mine."

"I feel that we are at an impasse," he said as he pulled my hand away from his mouth.

"We are. The only thing that can be done is that we both promise to watch each other's backs. Agreed?"

"I already promised to protect you, I cannot change that promise."

I groaned. "We were four!"

"And I meant it. When I saw you covered in ogre's blood and crying in my father's arms, I had never felt such a strong protective urge in my life. It was like I was created simply to protect you." He shook his head. "I know that doesn't make sense to you, but that's how I feel."

"We can't be partners if you don't allow me to protect you with my life as well. Partners protect *each other*," I reminded him as I laid down beside him.

"Well then I guess we aren't partners," he said.

I turned and stared at him in alarm and disbelief. "What?" He smiled. "I guess I'm more like your bodyguard."

"No," I said adamantly. "You are not my bodyguard. I refuse to have a bodyguard. If you aren't my partner than you aren't anything," I said seriously though I felt fear shaking my hands.

Favian linked our hands that were touching on

the one side together and said, "We will always be partners, Marin. I shouldn't have to tell you that so many times."

I felt heat rushing to my face at our joined hands, but enjoyed the feeling too much to pull away. "Then stop this crazy bodyguard talk and let us be partners."

He closed his eyes and yawned. "Alright. Partners."

I tried to fight the yawn that was trying to come out, but it slipped past my lips and my eyelids grew heavy. "Finally, I won an argument."

"Don't let it go to your head," he whispered as he started to fall asleep.

I sadly pulled my hand from his to pull up the blanket at the bottom of the bed to cover us both and closed my eyes. "Stubborn Elf," I whispered as sleep pressed down upon me.

"Obstinate human," he whispered and then we both started snoring.

8

"Marin, have you seen Prince Favian? I can't…" Amile began as she opened my door and stepped inside my room.

I was still groggy with sleep and Favian was still completely asleep, so there was nothing I could do to hide the fact that we had shared a bed. It had been completely harmless, but Amile wouldn't know that from simply looking and even though I threw the covers back to reveal us both fully clothed, Favian's shirt was off, but he'd come to my room like that, I couldn't get a word out before she jumped to conclusions.

Amile screamed and then charged at me, trying to slap my face. "You evil temptress!" she screamed as she tried to hit me. "How dare you defile him and use your dirty, evil humanness to…"

"Amile, please calm down," Favian said as he woke up and figured out the situation. He was trying to get across the bed to intervene, but I was mad now and she was still slapping at my face.

I had been okay with her displeasure until she had started to insult me. Now I was really angry. I punched her in the face and knocked her to her butt. "Your ignorance was dismissed at first, but once you started insulting me you crossed the line. First, you had no right to barge into my room without my permission. Secondly, I did not lure him to my room. He came here willingly last night and knocked on *my* door."

"Marin…" Favian said. "That's not helping."

"Thirdly, I am not an evil temptress. We shared a bed and slept, nothing else. My virginity is still intact, thank you. Fourthly, if you ever call me an evil human or insult me because of my humanity again, I will kill you. Now, remove yourself from my quarters before I change my mind about showing you mercy," I finished.

She stood up and glared at me. I had to hand it to the girl, she was tough for getting punched and having someone threaten her life. "Who gave you that necklace?" she asked. "Was it Favian?"

"No, actually it was me," Maddock said from the doorway. "And obviously, I missed one hell of a party."

I grabbed Amile by the throat and pushed her backwards so that she stumbled out of my room. "I was being serious, Amile. Next time I will kill you."

Her face paled and I yanked Maddock inside the room and slammed my door shut. "What happened?" Maddock asked Favian.

I walked to my window and opened it, drawing in deep breaths to calm myself and keep the female emotions away. I could hear Favian updating Maddock on the events, but I couldn't look at them yet. I was upset, but not because she had assumed I was sleeping with Favian. I was upset because of the other things she had said. Why did it bother me that she thought I would have to be an evil temptress for Favian to share a bed with me? Was I that hideous?

"Marin, what's wrong?" Favian asked.

I shook my head and pushed the emotions down. "Nothing. Let's get our things and head out. The sooner we get to the Academy, the better."

Favian and Maddock looked at me and then shared a look with each other.

I ignored them and grabbed my bag, making sure I had everything and then put on my boots and strapped my sword on since I was already dressed. Favian and Maddock left me and I turned to look at myself in the full-length mirror Mother had forced me to put in my room. I stared at myself and couldn't see an ugly girl, but neither could I see a beautiful girl, or a beautiful Elf like Amile. Maybe she was right. Maybe I was too ugly for Favian or any other Elf to ever be interested in.

I shook my head at my ridiculousness and jogged out to the courtyard where Favian, Maddock, Father, Mother, and the horses were. Amile gave me a dirty look and then started to try to talk with Favian, but he spoke quickly and angrily to her, interrupting her and then gave her the bracelet she had given him. She spoke angrily back to him and then burst into tears and ran out of the courtyard. If I didn't hate the girl so much, I might have felt sorry for her.

I climbed onto Fire's back and waved to Maddock and Father. "Good bye. I'll see you soon."

Favian mounted Ice and cantered after me to catch up as we exited the gates and went on the main road. We cantered slowly for a few hours and then we slowed to a walk to preserve the horses, especially since we might need to escape from other Mercenaries.

"So, are you going to tell me what's bothering you or are you going to make me pester you again?" he asked me as he moved Ice closer to Fire.

"Am I ugly?" I asked him.

He stared at me with the most priceless stunned expression and asked, "What?"

"Am I ugly?" I asked again. "No," he said. "Why?"

"Do not lie to me. Am I ugly? I mean I know I am not beautiful, but do you think I'm unattractive?"

He stopped Ice, and Fire stopped beside him even though I hadn't given her a command. "What's going on? Why are you asking me this?"

"Please answer me. I must know. I promise I won't hold it against you if you think I'm hideous," I said pleadingly.

"You want the honest answer?" he asked.

I nodded.

He took a deep breath and then he said, "You are beautiful."

I groaned and squeezed my legs to make Fire go. "I hate when you lie to me."

He grabbed Fire's reins and stopped her so he could face me completely. "I am not lying, Marin. You are beautiful. You wanted my honest answer and that is what I gave you. I think that you are beautiful. I assumed you already knew that."

"I think you're crazy if you believe I am beautiful, but thank you."

"What brought this on?" he asked, releasing Fire's reins. "Amile seemed so sure that you wouldn't sleep with me unless I was some evil temptress, so I assumed it was because I was ugly," I answered him honestly. I sighed. "She was probably just upset since she fancies you and she thought I had defiled you."

Favian went back to being silent as we continued on our way. We kept focused on everything around us, looking for any sign of danger. We left the forest, passed the fields and made it to the gate unscathed.

"What are you doing back so soon?" the gatekeeper asked when he saw me.

"I escaped from the dungeons of the Elves and they decided to let me come finish my training," I said, teasing Favian.

Favian rolled his eyes. "We had a change of heart and decided that it was only right to let her finish her schooling since she'd worked so hard."

The gatekeeper nodded in agreement. "I feel the same way. Alright boys, let 'em in."

We walked through the gate and into the town and then continued on our way to the shops. We stopped at the butcher just long enough for me to purchase a piece of barbecued beef. I ate it happily as we made our way through the rest of the town. "This is so delicious," I said around a bite in my mouth.

Favian looked at me with disgust and shook his head. "You're foul."

I smiled with beef in my teeth. "Thank you."

He shook his head at me and then turned his attention back to protecting me. "Who approaches the gate?" asked the back guard.

"Favian and Marin," Favian called out. "Please grant us permission to pass to the Academy."

"Permission granted."

The gate opened and we cantered out onto the main street and towards the Academy. "So far, so good," I whispered as I patted Fire's neck.

"Don't get complacent," Favian said.

"I know, I know," I muttered.

The forest converged around the road and we galloped two more miles towards the Academy when we spotted the trap. Thankfully it was midday so we had plenty of light to see the trap strung across the road ahead of us. It was simple trip wire which our horses would pull with their hooves when we ran across the road.

"Innocent lives could have been taken by this trap," Favian said angrily.

We dismounted and surveyed the sides of the road to look for any other traps, finding three before we finally made it around. "How did they know I was even coming back to the Academy?" I asked.

"These traps weren't for you," he said quietly.

I turned and stared at him in shock as I comprehended what he was saying. They were traps set for him. They were going to capture him in order to lure me to them. It would have worked too. If I heard that Favian was being held prisoner and they wanted to trade me for him, I would go in an instant. "Well, we know they're smart," I grunted.

"So, you're admitting that you would have fallen for their trap knowing they would have probably just killed us both in the end?" he asked me.

I nodded. "Yes, and you would do the same."

He ignored me since he knew I was right. We were each other's weakness and if they grabbed one of us, they would get both of us. Most Mercenaries didn't have partners for that very reason, but having grown up together with his overprotectiveness had made the transition to partner inevitable.

We finally made it to the Academy and were ushered inside immediately. As we untacked the horses Macon came into the stables. "Good to see you, Marin."

I smiled. "Thank you, sir. I'm glad to be back and ready to finish up this year."

"So, you are ready to complete your final test then?" he asked. I nodded. "Yes."

He looked at Favian. "Are you ready?" Favian nodded. "I am, sir."

Macon smiled. "Good. Get some food and rest today. We will brief everyone tomorrow morning on the plan and then execute it that day."

"One day?" Favian asked in shock. "I thought we were going to wait?"

"We were, but the attack at the school shows just how serious these people are. We must act quickly and we must find out who is after Marin before it is too late," Macon said seriously.

I nodded. "I completely agree. I am tired of being scared and looking at every leaf like it could be hiding a kidnapper."

"Finish up and then head to the food hall," Macon said. "And Marin, it truly is good to have you back at the Academy."

It was the nicest thing Macon had ever said to me and it filled my heart with joy. I finished putting away Fire's tack and then followed Favian to the food hall where we waited in line with everyone else for lunch.

"Marin!" Micah called happily. "I am so glad to see you. I couldn't believe my eyes when I saw them taking your unconscious body away."

"Yes, that was fun," I said sarcastically as Favian purposefully avoided eye contact with me. "How have things been since I left?" Micah smiled. "They haven't been the same without you around, but it has still been very busy. Everyone has been preparing for the final test and I have to say I'm really looking forward to it."

"We all are," I said with a smile.

The line moved forward and Micah waved good bye to us as he left the food hall. "He seemed different," Favian whispered.

"What?" I asked. "How?"

He shrugged. "I can't really say. It was just a feeling I got when he was talking to you."

"You are being super paranoid," I said angrily. "He has been a good friend to both of us the past six years."

"I know," he said as he grabbed a plate. "Just remember that our enemies could be anyone."

"Even you?" I asked him with cross eyes.

He rolled his eyes at me. "Yes, even I could be a potential enemy."

"You are so dramatic sometimes."

"You need to keep guard at all times," Favian said seriously.

I took the plate back from the chef and asked, "Is this safe? Or have you poisoned it?"

The chef waved his ladle at me. "Watch your tongue, girl."

"Blame Favian, sir. He's the one telling me I need to be on guard from everyone."

"He is right that you need to be on guard, but one must not forget their comrades when enemies are after them. Your comrades may be the only ones who can save you," the chef said as he served the student behind me.

We ate our food and then I went to my dorm and took a nap. Favian's protectiveness had exhausted me. I had planned to take a short nap, but ended up sleeping through the night and waking up just as the morning call rose in the school. I rolled out of bed and screamed when I tripped and fell on top of Favian.

"What the hell are you doing here?" I asked him.

"You left the door unlocked," he chastised me as he roused himself from sleep. "And I wanted to be sure you were safe and the only way to do that was to sleep in your dorm."

"You cannot sleep in my dorm. Rumors will spread and..."

"I do not care about *rumors*," he said angrily. "I care about your safety."

I rubbed the sleep from my eyes and sighed. "I'm sorry I snapped at you, but you scared me."

"Better I scare you than an enemy."

I resisted the urge to kick him and quickly grabbed

my belt with my sword and throwing knives. He followed me out the door and as I expected students were already out and we received quite a few stares. I held my head high, refusing to be embarrassed since nothing had happened and walked confidently to the food hall to eat breakfast.

Usually, people tried to keep their voices down when gossiping, but today it seemed that no one cared. Wild gossip raged within the food hall about my night with Favian, but unlike with Amile, the people here assumed that he had pushed himself on me. For some reason that made my day a little bit brighter and put a smile on my face.

"You seem chipper for someone who is being gossiped about," Favian commented as we exited the food hall.

"Well, it's not bad gossip for me," I said with a smile. "You're incorrigible," he muttered.

We headed to the covered fighting ring and thankfully found it empty. The arena was filled with a soft dirt that was easy to move around on and didn't hurt you when you were thrown on it or tackled.

"You want easy or hard?" Favian asked as we stretched. "Hard," I said as I stretched my hamstrings. "No weapons though."

He gave me the do-you-think-I'm-stupid look and then took a ready stance in the center of the ring. I met him, mimicking his stance. "You attack," he said with a smile.

I took a deep, calming breath and then attacked him. My attacks were essentially pointless since he blocked each and every one of them, but it was still

140

good to practice the punches. He kicked at me and I blocked it with my leg while trying to hit him with my hand. He let me attack him for forty minutes and then switched from defensive to offensive.

I blocked as many hits as I could, but he still managed to land a few on my ribs. His fist flew just passed my face, barely missing my cheek as I leaned backwards to avoid it. I hadn't known we had attracted an audience until I heard the reaction to the near hit. For some reason, the audience made me fight harder and I could see the frustration in Favian's face as he tried to hit me and kick me, but none landed.

Finally, he grew tired of the hand-to-hand combat and tackled me to the ground. The air rushed out of me in a loud grunt when we landed, but I immediately brought my knees up to keep him from pinning me. I pulled my leg up slowly from between his legs and then used it to propel him up and off of me.

Some of the crowd cheered while others booed. I ignored them all to focus on Favian. It wasn't often that we got to goof around like this and I was enjoying myself. I lunged forward and slowed to use a low kick, but Favian caught me off guard with a downward punch that caught me in the cheek and knocked me onto my back. My vision blurred and bright lights danced across my vision as I groaned in pain. He really was playing hard because he hadn't held anything back from that punch. I'd been punched by him before, but never in the face. It was a whole other type of pain that I was not used to.

I shook my head to clear it and stood up to face

him again despite my throbbing cheek and the embarrassment I felt at getting caught so off guard. I took a step to engage him again when Master Martin's whistle pierced the noise of the crowd and brought me to a halt.

"You're supposed to be resting," he chastised Favian and me. "Not fighting each other."

"We are resting," I said with a smile. "We're sparring, not fighting."

"Go to your dorms," he told everyone. "Today is a day for meditating and preparation mentally for the upcoming final test."

"Yes, sir," Favian said as he grabbed my arm and pulled me towards the exit to keep me from talking.

"I don't want to meditate in my dorm," I complained to Favian as we walked towards it.

"Just stay silent until we get to your dorm," he said as he looked around nervously.

"You're not coming into my dorm again," I said seriously.

"Yes, I am and there's nothing you can do to stop me," he answered in his Prince's voice. It was the voice that told me not to even try to argue or he'd tie me up and throw me over his shoulders. He had done it once and I did not want to relive that embarrassing moment again so I followed his orders and ignored the curious stares of the other students as we walked into my dorm and Favian shut and locked my door behind us.

I sat down on my bed, feeling tired and still shaky from the hit that Favian had landed and took deep, slow breaths. Favian squatted down in front of me and turned my head with his fingertips against my chin.

142

"How does your face feel?"

"Like I got kicked by a horse," I answered truthfully.

"I'm sorry, Marin. I thought you were going to block it. I would have held back if I had known you would miss." He probed it and I hissed in pain.

"Don't apologize. It's my fault for not paying attention," I whispered as he continued to inspect the swollen spot.

"Do you still have some of that pain medication?" he asked as he looked underneath my bed.

"Yes, it should be in the leather pouch," I said as I lay down and tried to hide the blush now on my face. I did not like these new feelings which made me feel uncomfortable when Favian touched me in certain ways. I'd been his friend for too long for stupid things like this to bother me!

"Here it is," he said as he pulled the leather pouch out and scooted out from under my bed with it. He opened the bottle and said, "Open your mouth and stick out your tongue."

I did as he asked and he sprinkled some of the pain medication onto my tongue. I let it dissolve and then closed my eyes. "Thanks."

"So, be honest with me," he said quietly. "How do you feel about the mission?"

"I am terrified, but know it needs to be done and I am really looking forward to it all being over," I answered him. "How are you feeling?"

"Worried because I am scared something is going to go wrong and using you as bait will be your death sentence. There are too many variables and too many

143

things that could go wrong. Especially, since we are facing other Mercenaries that attended this school and learned everything we did from the same teachers."

"If they do capture me you have to promise me something, okay?"

"What?" he asked skeptically.

"If they try to lure you with me, don't do it. Promise me you will stay with the Academy and work with them to figure out how to rescue me. Please promise me that you won't come after me yourself."

Favian looked down at his hands. "I can't promise that, Marin."

I slid out of the bed to sit on the floor in front of him. "Favian, you have to promise me. I will not be able to focus on the mission tomorrow if you don't promise me that you will be safe if something happens and I'm kidnapped. Please. Please promise me."

He met my eyes and shook his head. "I won't promise you that, Marin because I couldn't keep that promise. I promised you I would protect you and if you get kidnapped, I will do everything that I can to get you back."

"You will be walking to your own death!" I yelled at him. "You can't do that. It's better if one of us dies, not both. If I die, few will mourn about it and then be done. If you die, your Kingdom will lose its Prince and lose what would have been an amazing Kingdom once you were in control. Your father and mother will be crushed. Your people will be crushed. You cannot die!"

"I would be crushed if you died!" he screamed at me. "Don't you understand that? If you died, I would never forgive myself. Never!"

I knew he felt strongly for me as friends, but his declaration shocked me. "Favian," I whispered.

He shook his head and wrapped me in a tight hug. "I will not allow you to die. I would rather I died. If you died, I wouldn't care about my Kingdom or my parents. Everything would lose its meaning without you breathing in this world."

I pulled back from him so we could face each other again. "You're making it sound like you love me," I joked with him. "I understand you would be upset, but eventually my memory would fade and—"

"Never," he said fervently. "I will never forget about you. You don't get it, do you?" He shook his head and laughed miserably. "No, of course you don't." He grabbed my chin and stared into my eyes. "I will not make you that promise. I will promise you instead that I will travel to the ends of the earth to save you when you are in trouble. You are my best friend and my partner."

I didn't have any words to respond to him so I hugged him again and sighed. "You are such a stubborn Elf."

He laughed. "I learn from the best."

We sat in each other's arms for a few more minutes and then I grabbed my sword and knives and started cleaning them to give my hands other things to do to avoid letting them touch Favian in the strange ways that I was now wanting to.

We sat on the floor next to each other and cleaned our weapons and reminisced about prior events and laughed. It was calming and exactly what I needed the night before I was to be used as bait.

The time passed and we went to the food hall for dinner and then returned to my dorm to talk and tease each other more. I knew he was trying his hardest to keep my mind off of tomorrow's plan and I appreciated it more than he would ever know. After the sun set and the reality set in, I lay in my bed going over the various mistakes that could happen to try to plan out my actions in those events. I was convinced I'd thoroughly worked through every possible situation and yawned loudly.

"I'm going to get some sleep," I said as I pulled the blankets up around my shoulders.

He nodded. "It is getting rather late." He double checked the locks on the door, set our swords on each side of the bed so we could grab them in case we were attacked and then blew out the lamp on my side table. He climbed into bed with me and wrapped his arms around me, pulling me tight against his body. "One more day and then we will be free to take jobs as Mercenaries and live our lives as we are supposed to. One more day and then we will be adults."

"One more day," I whispered sleepily.

He kissed the back of my head and whispered, "Sleep well, Marin. I am here and I will protect you while you sleep."

"Only while I sleep?" I asked in a fake shocked tone as I pondered over the kiss he'd placed on my head. Had it been friendly? Was he actually interested in me?

"While you breathe," he said. "Or until I stop."

I rolled over to face him and stared at his outline

in the dark. "I will ensure you live the longest."

He tucked a strand of my hair behind my ear and my heart began beating faster. "We will agree to disagree on the matter. Now, go to sleep."

I relaxed and closed my eyes, but then asked a question I was dying to know. "Are there any at the court that you are planning on courting when we return?" I knew he didn't like Amile so I wasn't thinking about her, but the other hundred beautiful Elf women that were eligible and would die for his attention and affection.

"There is one," he said. "But now is not the time to discuss that. Now is the time for sleep."

"Right," I muttered as I rolled over and put my clenched fists under my armpits.

"Are you jealous?" he asked with humor in his voice.

My mouth gaped open. "Of course not!" I said angrily. "How could you even ask such a preposterous thing?!"

He laughed and kissed the back of my head again. "Okay, go to sleep."

I closed my eyes and relaxed with him at my back. Finally, my emotions settled down enough and I slept in his arms.

9

"Marin! Favian! Time to get up!" Micah called through my door.

"We're up," I called back just as Favian opened the door to step outside.

"Morning," Favian said.

"You look awfully dreary for the day of your final," Micah said cheerfully.

"I seem to be the only one who truly values her life so of course I am dreary."

"Don't start with that again," I said as I walked out behind him. "I get to go shopping today, aren't you at least excited for me?"

Favian rolled his eyes and walked on to the food hall. "What's wrong with him?" Micah asked.

I patted his back. "He has always been very over protective and for the first time there is nothing he can do except pray and worry that everything will go okay."

"But things never go as planned," Micah

whispered. I smiled. "Exactly."

The Academy was bustling with activity and despite my fear I was smiling widely as we ate and then hurried to meet Macon and the Masters in the covered arena. I sat down beside Favian and nudged his shoulder gently with mine, getting a small smile from him in return. Victory!

Macon faced us all and gave us the serious face. The one that said sit down, shut up and pay attention. "As you all know, this test will be much different and much harder than the ones in previous years. This test will involve the true danger of one of our own and though our objective is to locate the kidnappers and obtain information from them as to who is behind this, our main priority is Marin's safety."

"Yes, sir," All twelve of the other sixth years said in unison. "Now, we will be separating you into several different teams with various objectives. Marin and Favian you two have your own objectives, so please follow me. The rest of you, please listen to Masters Martin and Sean as they break you up into your groups and explain all of your directives. We leave in one hour."

My heartbeat doubled and my breathing quickened at the nearness of our escapade. Favian and I followed Macon to his office and sat down in chairs across from his desk.

"How are you feeling?" Macon asked me. "Nervous, but ready," I answered him honestly.

"Good," he said with a nod of his head. "You?" he asked Favian.

"Anxious for it to be over," he said as he sat in his chair as though he didn't have a care in the world. I hated how he could look completely calm when he was seething underneath. I couldn't hide my emotions even when I tried.

"We are going to have you two ride in first and tie your horses up at the tavern. Then you two will shop around the town square. I don't care if you buy items or if you just browse, but make it look realistic."

"It will be," I said with a smile. "I am in need of some supplies that I know I can get from a few of the vendors."

"Good," Macon said with a nod of his head. "Favian, I want you to be alert, but look calm."

"Done," Favian said with a nod of his head. "Where will everyone else be?"

"Some will be fellow shoppers while others will be on rooftops and others still disguised as beggars. If you are attacked, I want you to apprehend at least one person and then whistle as loudly as you can. If you are in danger, I want you to scream as loud as you can Marin, you understand?"

I nodded. "Yes, sir."

"Some of the people after you are fellow Mercenaries and I assume that all of those after you now will know that you are a student of the Academy, so you can't play innocent girl this time. Go saddle up your horses and get ready for departure. Stay safe and good luck," he said as he ushered us out the door.

Favian and I hurried to the stables and brushed and tacked our horses in record time. I mounted Fire and Favian moved close next to me so that our legs were touching. "Keep your eyes open and please listen to me if I tell you to move or something. Okay?"

I patted his knee and smiled. "Yes, sir."

"Are you ready?" Masters Sean and Martin asked as the rest of the sixth years entered the stables.

We nodded our heads and Master Sean said, "Remember to look up and behind you."

"Yes, sir," I said.

"We hope you pass," Master Martin said. "Now go out there and kick some kidnapper butt."

I squeezed Fire's sides and we galloped out of the school and towards the town. Favian stayed glued to my side, scanning our surroundings for danger and listening ahead for any warning sounds. The road was clear of traps this time and we made it to the town unscathed. The gatekeeper waved us in and it was clear he knew what was happening. We walked the horses to the tavern and I was shocked to see that the town was filled with people.

"What's going on?" I asked a passerby.

"Town festival," he said with a smile. "Everyone from miles away is here to participate."

"Wonderful," Favian said irritably.

We checked the horses to ensure they were tied for an easy escape if we needed their assistance and then set out into the crowd of people headed towards the town square. Favian stuck close by me, his arm constantly touching mine as we walked and did as he was supposed to do, appear as though he were bored and being forced to accompany me to the market. I put on my happy, girly face and started stopping at all of the vendors with a plan to visit every single one.

Every time I turned my back to the crowd to look at a vendor's items Favian stood with his back to mine so he would protect me from any arrows that might have been aimed at my back. The first fifteen minutes went by boringly and then a troupe of performers set up a stage in the center of the square and I grabbed Favian's hand, dragging him behind me as I moved closer to get a better view. "Slow down," he said with a laugh as I pushed our way through the crowd.

I finally found a vantage point I liked and came to a stop. "I love troupes," I said giddily to Favian.

He moved to stand directly behind my back and set his arms on top of my shoulders to look as though he were leaning on me. "There are two suspicious looking men to our left. One is tall and built like a wall and the other is in a hooded cloak so I cannot see his face, but he has a rapier at his side."

"A fencer? That's insulting," I said as I smiled and pretended that we were talking about normal teenage life, not possible kidnappers.

The troupe came out onto the stage and I stared in awe at the bright colors of their costumes. "We come today to tell you a tale. A tale of love and a tale of tragedy."

"This sounds uplifting," Favian whispered sarcastically.

I smacked his hand on my left shoulder and turned my attention back to the troupe who had started to dance on the stage. I stood mesmerized and transfixed as they danced a story of love which ended with an untimely death for the girl. It was beautiful, graceful and much too close to home for comfort. Nonetheless, I clapped exuberantly when they finished and cheered, "Bravo!"

The crowd began dispersing and Favian and I dispersed with them to the last vendor I had been at. I purchased a bag of white shells and some small rope I could use to make a necklace with. We went to the next vendor, having to make our way through the crowd which had dispersed to visit the vendors just as we had.

I had never seen the town so full of people and I felt excited and frightened at the same time. I saw a few of the other sixth years and Micah ran into my shoulder as he passed by, but besides the men that Favian had spotted, nothing seemed out of the ordinary.

Perhaps they wouldn't be at the town today. Maybe they were waiting in the woods again? I stopped at a vendor who had exquisite jewelry and stared in awe at a beautiful blue sapphire bracelet.

"Would you like to hold it?" the vendor asked with a smile. "Oh, I couldn't," I said as I took a step back.

Favian took the bracelet and examined it thoroughly. "These are exquisite gemstones," he said to the vendor who bowed his head in thanks. "How much?"

"Favian," I said with wide eyes. "You can't buy that."

"One hundred," the vendor said.

Favian pulled out his money pouch and started to count out pieces.

"Favian," I said again. "I was just looking, you don't —"

"Do you want it?" he asked.

I bit my lip and chewed on it. "Yes, but…"

"But nothing," he said as he handed his money to the vendor. "Thank you," the vendor said. "May it bring you many joys." Favian clipped the bracelet onto my wrist and whispered,

"You must have something beautiful and girly to wear, even while on missions as a Mercenary or Protector. Besides, I think it looks great on you."

"It's so beautiful," I said as I held my wrist up and turned it in the sun. I turned and threw my arms around Favian's neck and then kissed his cheek quickly. "Thank you."

"You're welcome," he said happily. "Now, let's move on to the next vendor."

I stopped at the leather vendor and bought a small pouch for the bracelet in case I had to take it off for some reason and then bought leather to mend my saddle and leather to make a new pouch for medicines.

The day seemed to be completely uneventful and as midday hit, I had to beg Favian to let me buy food to ease my rumbling stomach. We stood in line at the food vendor nearest our current route and I ate the smoked turkey leg with extreme pleasure as Favian ate a large root of some kind.

"If nothing happens today does that mean we pass our test?" I asked him.

Favian laughed. "Probably not, but don't be complacent. They may be waiting for that to happen to attack."

"I'm not complacent," I said as I held up my new bracelet and admired its beauty again.

"I'm glad you like it so much," he said. "It is quite difficult to find you a gift you enjoy."

"That's not true," I said defensively. "I loved the throwing knives you got me last year." I patted my belt. "I use them almost every day."

He rolled his eyes. "I mean gifts that are not for our jobs."

I shrugged. "There aren't usually things I want. This is just so beautiful," I said. "I really do love it, but one hundred is a lot. I'm sure the vendor would let you return it..."

"No," Favian said. "I bought you it and you shall wear it the rest of your life."

I smiled. "Yes, sir."

We finished eating and started shopping again. Favian bought a few items, but the pack he brought to carry our purchases was getting pretty full. The sun began to set as we came to the last vendors. A fight broke out near the vendor and Favian turned to examine it as I examined a strange medallion in the hands of the vendor. "What is that?" I asked.

Favian glanced at the medallion and then turned his attention back to the fight and the crowd it was drawing.

"This is a very special medallion," the vendor said with a bright smile. "Would you care to hold it? Some say it gives them a preview of their future."

"I'm all out of money," I said sadly. "I wouldn't want to break it."

"Nonsense!" the vendor said. "I insist that you hold it. A beautiful Mercenary like you should see her future. I promise the medallion won't bite you, it has no teeth. See?" he said as he turned the medallion over in his hands so I could examine it.

I laughed. "Alright." I held my hand out and he set it in my palm and then quickly wrapped the strap around my wrist. "What the..." I began as his movement shocked me, but then some strange feeling spread through me and the world began spinning.

"Marin!" Favian yelled.

I tried to move to him, but the medallion felt as though it were burning into my skin and all of my energy was draining from me. I hit the ground on my side and watched in fear and rage as three men fought against Favian, keeping him away from me. I tried to scream to alert the others, but it was all I could do to keep my eyes open and breathe.

Favian killed one of the men, but the other two continued their assault on Favian, pushing him further and further away from me. A tall, muscular man picked me up and tossed me over his shoulder. "Time to go," he said in a deep voice.

"MARIN!" Favian screamed as the man began running. I watched as Favian killed the two attacking him and then tried to run through the crowd, only to be blocked by the swarm and held further and further back. The man with the rapier stepped forward and stabbed Favian in the stomach with a dagger.

"Fav...ian." I tried to yell, but ended up saying it softly as I lost my fight to stay conscious and darkness surrounded me.

"Wakey wakey," an unfamiliar male voice said from nearby. "Time to wake up, Marin."

"Favian," I whispered as I opened my eyes and tried to sit up. "Favian!"

"Calm down, girl. Your friend isn't here. I'm sure he is safe at the Academy being tended to by the healer by now."

I sat upwards and realized I was bound by ropes. "Where are we?" I asked as my eyesight returned and I could finally see the room I was in. It was a small wooden shack with a bed, two chairs and a fireplace. I was on the bed, tied up tightly and a man was sitting in a chair across the room from me. The man was ugly with three front cracked teeth and a long scar on the left side of his face.

He smiled. "We are at a halfway point. Shortly you will be picked up by a different person who will take you to your final destination."

"Why are you helping this person kidnap me?" I asked angrily as I slowly started twisting my wrist to escape from the ropes tying me. Thankfully it was the exact type of binding that Masters Sean and Martin had been working with me on. The loop around my throat tightened slightly, but I had enough room still to breathe freely.

"It's just a paying job," the man said. "And stop trying to escape from the ropes."

I slipped the ropes down my wrist a little farther and asked, "What does this person have planned for me?"

He shrugged. "I don't know and I don't care. My job is just to get you here and wait for the next one to get you." I almost got the loop off my wrist, but the man stood up and walked to me, dangling the medallion from his hand. "I told you to stop trying to get free. Now I'm going to have to use this."

"What is that?" I asked. "Why does it hurt me?"

He pushed the rope higher up my wrist, wrapped the strap around my wrist and pressed the medallion into my palm. "I don't know. I just know it knocks you out and makes it much easier to move you."

I tried to fight it. I tried to at least let go of the stupid medallion, but all I could do was faint again from the pain and energy sapping power the medallion had over me. Why? Why did it work against me and not these other men?

I woke up lying across the back of a horse, with my hands tied to my feet so that if I flung myself backwards off of the horse, I would just slide underneath its belly. If it had been Fire whose back I was on, I would have done it and then gotten the rope off of her butt, which she would have then stepped over so I would be free. Sadly, this was not Fire and I had no idea if this horse would kick me or trample me if I tried it.

I lifted my head slightly so I could look at my surroundings to try to figure out where I was, but nothing looked familiar about this area. It was heavily wooded and the road was dirt, but I didn't believe I had ever traveled this way before. When I managed to get free, I would have to ride in the opposite direction and hope I could find a familiar landmark. Unfortunately, I had no idea how long I'd been out or how far we'd traveled.

"You awake finally?" a new male voice asked.

"I need to use the restroom," I muttered sleepily.

"Sure thing," he said. I kept my head down and pretended to still be weak as he untied me from the horse and pulled me down to my feet. He held the rope which was still tied to my hands and led me into the forest off the side of the road. I stumbled forward like I was weak and leaned against the tree he was tying the rope to. "Do your business and let's go," he said as he walked backwards ten feet.

"Can I have some privacy?" I asked as I started pushing my pants down.

He shook his head. "Nope."

I groaned and walked around to the other side of the tree so I was at least partially hidden from him as I went pee. "Do you have any water or food?" I asked as I pulled my pants up and walked around the tree to him.

"In my pack," he said as he started untying the rope from the tree. I waited until his back was completely turned to me and then jumped up onto his back, looped my hands over his head and started choking him with the rope between my wrists. He grabbed at my wrists to pull them forward, but I planted my elbows in his back and leaned back to keep the pressure on. He spun around, hitting my side into the tree, but I held on, refusing to be dislodged and lose my one chance at getting free.

He reached for his sword and I used my right leg to hit his hand and then held his arm down with my leg wrapped around it. He started slowing as the lack of oxygen took effect. Seconds later he dropped to his knees and then fell on his face. I didn't want to kill him, but I had to hold the rope around his throat a few seconds longer to ensure he wasn't faking.

I released him, checked to ensure his pulse was still beating, grabbed a dagger from his belt and cut the ropes off of my hands. I couldn't have him following me right away, so I tied his hands behind his back and then tied his feet to his hands in a hog tie variation that was very difficult to free yourself from. I took his belt with his sword and daggers and strapped it onto myself and then mounted his horse and squeezed my legs. The horse took off at a fast gallop and we headed back in the direction he'd taken me.

I rode for an hour and still nothing in the landscape changed and nothing looked familiar. Where was I? I wanted to save the horse's stamina, but at the same time I wanted to be sure I rode far away from the people after me. I slowed the horse to a trot and opened the saddle bags in search of food and water, luckily finding both. I chewed on the dried meat like a starving dog and guzzled the water down. I really wished I knew how long I'd been out, but the only ones who knew that were the ones I was trying to avoid.

I searched for the sun and finally figured out I was currently heading South, but since I had no idea if we had headed West first or East or Northeast I had no way of knowing exactly which way to head. I growled in frustration and felt like stabbing someone. Maybe I should have killed the man instead of tying him up.

"You think Kristof will make it without any

problems from that girl?" someone asked from around the bend in the road.

I jerked my horse off the road and hid as the men came within view. There were three of them, the cloaked fencer, the man with the scar and the large man all rode together down the road, looking smug. I wanted to attack them, but I was too outnumbered.

"He'd better not have any problems with her. He has the medallion if she starts getting feisty," the scar man said.

"Does anyone know why the medallion works on her and not us?" the large man asked.

"The fencer knows," scar man said. "But since he doesn't talk, it's a mystery to me still."

My horse must have felt lonely or known the other horses because when they were almost out of sight he neighed loudly. "You idiot," I grumbled as I kicked him and we bounded out of the forest and onto the road. I kicked him again, forcing him into a gallop in the opposite direction of the men and hoped they wouldn't catch me.

"Get her!" scar man yelled.

I urged the horse to go faster, but their horses were steadily catching up to us. "Dammit can't you go any faster?!" I screamed at the horse. The scarred man pulled up on my left side and reached out for my horse's reins, but I steered my horse to the right, avoiding his hand and then pulled a dagger from the belt. "Just let me go!" I yelled at him.

"Come on girl, this isn't personal it's just business. We aren't here to kill you," he said as he steered his horse closer to mine.

I held the dagger sideways in my left hand, preparing to slice at him if he got too close, but he was the least of my worries as the scarred man yelled, "Whoa," and the horse I was riding came to an abrupt halt.

"Thistles!" I screamed angrily as I hopped off the horse and started running through the woods.

"You can't run forever!" scarred man yelled.

"I can run a lot longer than you!" I yelled back as I turned left and headed South parallel to the road as I tried to outrun them. Unfortunately, the cloaked fencer had galloped ahead and swerved off the road into the forest ahead of me and leapt from his horse to pin me to the ground. I tried to get out from under him and stab him, but he was incredibly strong for such a thin man and held me down.

"Get the medallion," he said in a loud, deep voice.

His voice seemed familiar, but I couldn't place it. I tried to look at his face, but the cloak hung down so I couldn't see him. "Who are you?" I asked softly.

"Just a Mercenary doing his job," he replied.

"Please let me go. Please. I haven't done anything wrong and I don't deserve this."

"Most do not deserve what happens to them," he said as he was handed the medallion by the scarred man. I thrashed against him, but scar man held me down as the fencer started wrapping the medallion's strap around my wrist. He noticed the sapphire bracelet and took it off.

"Leave it!" I yelled at him. "Do not take that from me!" I yelled as I tried to strike him and get out of the scarred man's hold.

He ignored me, put it in his coin pouch and then pressed the medallion against my wrist as he tied it. I screamed in anger, but the medallion forced me into unconsciousness again.

I woke up three more times and they let me eat, drink and use the restroom, but then they were quick to use the medallion again to keep me sedated. I didn't know if hours, days, or weeks had passed since they'd taken me from Favian. All I knew was I planned to kill them all as soon as I could and the cloaked man was my first target since he had taken my bracelet from me.

I tried to fight them every opportunity I had, but they worked together and I was no match against three skilled Mercenaries. By the fourth time I woke up my fighting spirit had dwindled and I had started to give in to my fate. I felt like crying, but refused to do so in front of these men. I would hold my female emotions in until I was alone.

The scenery changed from forest to mountains to valleys of lush green grass. We stopped at several inns, but our final stopping place was a giant castle owned by a human whose name they kept hidden from me. Apparently, the human had been run out by rogue Mercenaries years before and other Mercenaries had come and kicked them out. Now it served as a safe house and my prison.

"Finally, we made it," scar man said with relief. "Let's get her down to the dungeons and shackled quickly."

"I hope there's food. I'm starving," the large man said. "You're always hungry," scar man said with disbelief.

I had one last burst of spirit and I kicked scar man in the chest when he untied me from the horse and I tried to run, but the cloaked man grabbed me and foiled my escape once again.

"I'm going to kill you," I said to him seriously. "I don't care if it's three years or ten years from now, but I will find you and kill you."

He said nothing as usual and carried me into the castle and then down the stairs to the dungeon which was littered with bones. It hadn't been used in years and I had to hope they put me in a cell with rusty chains that I could break. Sadly, they searched through each until they found good chains and locked me up in them.

"Food," I whispered.

"Fetch her food," scar man said to the large man.

"Okay," he said giddily as he went off in search of the kitchen and storage.

"Now if you are real nice, we will keep the medallion off of you, but if you try to act up, I'll strap it to your arm again without a second thought," scar man warned me.

"Couldn't you at least have had the decency to kill me instead of dragging me here to my death? As a fellow Mercenary, I would have given you that bit of respect," I grumbled.

"You are not a fellow Mercenary. You are a girl playing games and attempting to ruin what is a glorious line of work," he said angrily. "And if the fencer hadn't grabbed you when you tried to run the first time, you would have had an arrow in your back."

"I am not ruining anything. I have performed well

in various missions and proved myself worthy."

"You have only performed well because you had the Elf at your side. Without him, you are nothing."

It couldn't be true, but part of me felt that he was right. With Favian at my side we had accomplished everything, but what if I didn't have him? Could I perform just as well without him?

"Here," the large man said as he entered the dungeon and stepped inside my cell. "I had to go outside, but I found fresh apples and some dried meat."

"Thank you," I said as he set them in my outstretched hands. I knew most would think I was crazy for being nice to them, but they were honestly just obeying orders on a job and I couldn't fault them for that. I ate my food and then relaxed against the wall as the men went exploring. The cloaked man sat in a chair outside my cell and never moved and always kept his face hidden. "What are you?" I asked him. "Elf? Goblin? I know you aren't human."

"He's annoyingly quiet," scar man said as he came back down into the dungeon. "Though, I too am curious as to your origins."

The cloaked man remained quiet and still as though he couldn't hear them.

"Out with it, what are you?" the large man asked.

"He is not of your concern," a new voice said from somewhere in the dungeon. "I do not want my Mercenaries squabbling about nonsense. Is the girl here?"

"Yes, sir," scar man said.

"Then you are dismissed. Meet me in the dining

room and I shall give you your payments."

I was going to be alone with this new man? I didn't want the cloaked man to go. I wanted him to stay so I could get my bracelet back. "Wait!" I said angrily. "The cloaked man took something of mine and I want it back!"

"Come gentlemen, let's eat and have you on your way back home," the man said.

I jerked against the chains and tried to get them free of the wall, but that seemed to upset the cloaked man who opened the cell, strapped the medallion to me and pushed me down against the wall as I passed out. "I hate you," I whispered just before I went unconscious yet again.

10

I woke up with a pounding headache and a grumbling stomach. "I am really tired of that damn medallion," I said angrily.

"If you cooperate then there will be no need for its use anymore," said the voice of the man who had hired the Mercenaries. I turned my head to the left and found him sitting inside the cell on a wooden chair. He was handsome for a man in his late forties, but his eyes were dark and filled with hatred. He was an assassin, no doubt about it, not a Mercenary.

"What do you want?" I asked as I sat up and arranged the chains attached to my wrists comfortably.

"There are many things I want, Marin, but currently I have what I want. You," he said with a smug smile.

"Why? What do you want with me?" I asked as I looked around at the escape exits, which was sadly only the cell door behind his chair which was closed and probably locked.

"Sweetheart, who do you think you're talking to?

I'm not an idiotic bandit. I am a top rate Mercenary."

"You mean assassin," I corrected him.

He laughed. "Touché. Yes, I am an assassin, but you need not fear me, yet."

"What is your name?"

"Lawrence."

"Well, Lawrence, if you're going to kill me then just do it now," I said bitterly. "I have no information I can give you that I will reveal in torture."

"You are so ignorant, which is understandable since you are so young." He scooted forward and stared into my eyes. "You see my dear, I can learn whatever I want by torturing you. Truly I could learn the very blueprint of the Elven kingdom if I wanted to, but that is not why I have you."

"Why then? Why did you go through all of this trouble to kidnap me?" I asked feeling slightly more fearful.

"What do you remember about your life before the Elves found you?" he asked me as he played with the medallion, turning it over and over again.

"I remember I had a mother and father and we lived in a small town where I played with the headman's son often. I remember the ogres attacked and I watched as my family was murdered. Then I remember being carried by Cesar as he took me to the Elven Kingdom. Why? What does any of this have to do with why you kidnapped me?"

"You are the first girl to be allowed to attend the Academy, do you remember what you did to impress them enough to let you in?" he asked as he set the medallion on his lap and folded his arms across his chest, looking like he was chatting with his friend. He was dressed well and had a beautifully crafted pommel on his sword. None of it impressed me though.

"I fought against some of the students and won," I said nonchalantly. "I had been training privately with the male Elves since I came to their realm. I was not suited for the arts of women. Really it wasn't a fair battle since I'd been training with Elves and the students I fought were human."

"You fought fifth years and won in sword and hand to hand combat, correct?" he asked.

"Yes."

"And you hold back when you fight the other students so you don't make them feel bad that they were beat by a girl, right?"

"Not all the time," I said honestly. I never held back against Favian. "Mainly when I fight against the first or second years,"

I lied

"Isn't it true that you defeated over one hundred ogres by yourself at the Elven Kingdom?"

"How did you know about that?" I asked in shock.

"Is it also true that you have no recollection of the event?" he asked.

This guy knew way too much. I shut my mouth and stared blankly at him, refusing to confirm or deny his question. Just who was he?

"Playing mute will do you no good since I already know the answers," he said in a cheery voice. "Who do you think ordered the ogres to attack the Elves? I did."

"What is that medallion?" I asked him to change the subject. "This is an ancient artifact that was found in a tomb of the god and goddess, one that had been unvisited in several decades."

"What does it say?"

"It says, 'sent to protect the innocent, but reverting to the dark, use this to steal their light'."

"What the hell does that mean?" I asked angrily. "I'm not using evilness. I'm a Mercenary who protects everyone. I have never killed an innocent. I have never—"

"Do you take pleasure in killing ogres?" he asked me, cutting me off.

"Yes, but I have never killed an ogre who did not attack me first," I said defensively.

"But you wish you could, don't you? You wish you could obliterate every single ogre off of the face of the planet, right?"

How could I respond to that? "I'm not evil," I said softly.

He smiled. "Of course you're not. I never suspected you were.

"I'm just trying to get you to understand yourself."

"What is your end goal?" I asked him.

"To help you unlock your true destiny and for you to realize that you cannot continue as a Mercenary."

"I *am* a Mercenary," I said angrily. "I will complete the training. I will become one."

He stood up, flinging his chair backwards and stood in front of my face. "You are not capable of being a Mercenary. Mercenaries are *men*. You are a woman."

"Is that the real reason you kidnapped me? Because you don't want a woman to become a Mercenary?"

"Once the other women hear of this, there will be

more and they will want to train to be a Mercenary like you. Then the world will be overrun by second rate Mercenaries who constantly fail their missions and end up getting others killed simply because they didn't know when to stop playing dress up and keep their dresses and corsets on!"

"I am aware that the life of a Mercenary is not for women in general, but I am not an average woman. I am just as capable as any man."

"You are an abomination!" he screamed and then walked to his chair, righted it and sat down. He took several deep breaths to calm himself and then met my eyes. "You don't even know what you are, do you?"

"I'm abnormal, I'm aware of that," I said sadly. "I am much more skilled in manly arts than I am womanly arts.

I'm faster than a lot of other humans, but I believe that is simply because I train extremely hard and force myself to keep up with the Elves. I am strong, but not abnormally strong."

"Lie," he said. "You are abnormally strong. You just fail to understand how to unleash it."

"I have troubles lifting the feed sacks. How can you define that as abnormally strong?"

"You simply fail to understand how to unleash your true powers."

"You're crazy," I said seriously.

"I witnessed your attack on the ogres at the Elven Kingdom. You sliced through them like they were made of butter. No human is that strong."

"Are you trying to tell me that I'm not human?" I asked disbelievingly. This guy must be crazy.

"Not fully human," he said with a smirk.

"I bleed red. I faint when choked. I have stupid girly emotions. I trip and fall and scrap my knees. It took practice and training for me to gain muscle and be able to lift feed sacks. I can barely swing a mace. My parents were both human. I am human," I said through gritted teeth.

"You are part human," he agreed. "And those weren't your real parents." I couldn't think of anything to say that wouldn't piss him off so I just held my tongue. "If you were human this medallion wouldn't work on you," he said as he wiggled it.

"If you know so much, then why don't you tell me what I am?" I asked mockingly.

"I will not educate you so that you can unlock your true powers. I only want you to understand what you are and that you cannot be a Mercenary and you most certainly cannot become a Protector. Helping you unlock your true powers would be suicide on my part."

"Kidnapping me was suicide on your part. The Elves will hunt you down and slice you up into little tiny bits for kidnapping me. Unless I don't do it first that is."

He smiled. "I like your spunk, but your anger is misguided. I will release you as soon as you make a blood oath to stop pursuing the life of a Mercenary and agree to live as a lady in the Elven Kingdom."

I leapt to my feet and jerked on the chains, stretching to the end of them and pulling as hard as I could. "Never," I said as my blood began to boil. "I am a Mercenary and I always will be."

He shook his head and pushed the medallion against my arm. "Maybe after a few days without water or food you'll change your mind."

I wanted to curse at him. I wanted to slit his throat, but the damn medallion only forced me unconscious again.

"How are you today?" Lawrence asked. "Any change of heart?"

"Screw you," I mumbled as I woke up. "You might as well kill me."

"I have no intention of killing you, but if you refuse to see things my way I may be forced to."

"I'll never see things your way. Just kill me or put the medallion against my skin. I *am* a Mercenary."

"See this is part of the problem. Could you imagine if every woman thought it was okay to talk to men like this?"

"You aren't a man. You are a slimy, cold-hearted snake."

"I think more time unconscious will cure you."

"I think cutting off your head is the only way to cure you," I said angrily.

He pushed the medallion against my skin. "You have spirit, but I will break that soon."

"Feel like being a lady today?" he asked as I woke up again. "What day is it?" I asked him.

"You sleep for one day every time the medallion touches you. This is your fourth day at my castle. Plus, the medallion saps your strength." No wonder my throat was on fire for water and my stomach felt so empty. "So, do you feel like changing jobs yet?"

"I am a Mercenary," I whispered. "And once I get free, I will kill you."

"You sadden me, Marin. Truly you sadden me. If you go more than another day like this you will die."

"Then slit my throat now and put me out of my misery. My answer will not change."

"We shall see tomorrow," he said and tied the medallion around my neck. "Sweet dreams."

He left the cell and headed out of the dungeon area. I waited as long as I could and then whispered, "Fira."

The necklace Maddock had given me flared and the strap holding the medallion around my neck began sizzling. I took deep breaths and kept my eyes open to keep myself from passing out and finally the medallion fell to the ground and I was conscious. I was going to owe Maddock for his gift. I moved backwards to get away from the medallion and took inventory of my body. Half of my strength had been sapped by the medallion's contact, but I was pretty sure he wouldn't come back until the next day since he'd put the medallion on.

I had to escape. There had to be some way to get out. I leaned against the wall and looked around the cell. The only thing in the cell was the chair and that couldn't help me get out of the chains. I rubbed my neck and then a crazy idea crossed my mind. Could the necklace burn through the chains? There was only one way to find out so I held the chain up to my neck, leaned forward in case it got so hot it melted and the metal dripped and whispered, "Fira."

Bright light blinded me and I was forced to close my eyes and endure the heat as the necklace went to work. I dropped to my knees due to my weakness and when the metal shackle dropped to the floor, I bit my lip to keep from screaming in joy. I put the second one up and it too melted off. I relaxed against the wall a moment to conserve my strength and then went to the cell door and pushed it, sadly it was locked. I wondered if my necklace had a limit to how much it could be used and prayed silently that it would work at least long enough to get me out of the cell.

I pressed my neck against the side of the lock and whispered, "Fira," and then smiled when I heard it begin to sizzle. Footsteps clopped down the hallway above me and I knew my time was running out. The door swung open to my cell and I ran out to the side of the wall, which would hide me when Lawrence came downstairs. Why was he here already? Didn't he say I was out for an entire day each time he used the medallion? Why would he be back so soon?

The dungeon door opened and his boots clopped down the stairs in a giddy-like step. He walked down the steps and took four steps into the dungeon when he realized that my cell door was open and I wasn't in my restraints anymore. He ran into the cell, grabbing the medallion off of the floor and I ran up the stairs as fast as I could, shutting the dungeon door and trying to lock it. "Get back here!" he screamed. I ignored him, stopped trying to lock the door since I couldn't, and ran out the way the Mercenaries had brought me in, taking two steps out into the sunlight when Lawrence tackled me. I head butted him and rolled away, trying to run again with what little energy I had left.

He had the medallion in his hand and I knew if he used that, I would be done for and he would probably kill me. I ran out of the castle courtyard only to come up against a wall I didn't remember coming through. Why was my memory fragmented when I'd been awake?

"You have nowhere to run to and no one to help you," he said as he faced me. "I am very impressed that you got out. How did you do it?"

I ignored him as I surveyed my surroundings and searched for an escape option. I darted left, but apparently, he had been prepared for that and snatched me up, trying to place the medallion against my chest. I bit into his arm as hard as I could, piercing the skin and tasting blood. I ground my teeth together and he yelled in pain, dropping the medallion on the ground and losing his grip on the right side of my body. I tried to run, but he still had a hold of my left arm. I kicked him in the stomach as hard as I could, but he was prepared for that and flexed his stomach to take the impact.

He punched me in the face before I could block him and I dropped to my knees from the pain. It wasn't as hard as Favian's had been, but it was still a hell of a punch. I knew it was cruel and if my life hadn't been on the line, I never would have done it, but I punched him in his family jewels and ran like hell. I made it to the gate and had just started to pull it open when he grabbed my hair and slammed my face into the iron gate. "That hurt," he said angrily as he smashed my face against the gate again.

I elbowed him in the side, but it seemed I had pissed him off so much that pain wasn't an issue at the moment. He threw me to the ground and kicked me in the ribs. "You are a woman and it seems you need to be reminded of your place in the world of men." He grabbed my shirt and ripped it open, exposing my upper body and stomach. I tried to get away from him, but I barely had any strength and I couldn't escape him. He pulled at my pants and I kicked him in the nose as hard as I could when he let up on my legs.

He growled angrily and punched me in the face, making me gasp in pain and making my head spin. He started to move towards me and I did the only thing I could think of in the situation, I brought my knee up into his genitals as hard as I could.

He screamed in pain and punched me in the face again, this time clearly as hard as he could. "That was dirty and you know it," he growled. "Now, I'm going to make you pay." He straddled my hips and wrapped his hands around my throat, choking me.

I clawed at his hands and punched him in the sides and arms, but he held on, refusing to let me go. My vision started to blur and my ears began to ring as I lost consciousness for the last time.

"Marin!" I heard Favian yell.

I closed my eyes and prayed that he was okay. I hadn't wanted to die, but hallucinating hearing the sound of his voice was at least a small and strange happiness.

The man's hands were removed from my throat

and I was able to gasp in some air. I took in large, burning gulps of air and opened my eyes to find the cloaked man fighting with Lawrence. Why was the cloaked man fighting him? I didn't need to stick around to find out. I stood up and limped as quickly as I could out the gate and started down the road. I glanced back to see the cloaked man fighting hand to hand with Lawrence and starting to lose.

"Come back here!" Lawrence yelled and then started running from the cloaked man after me. The cloaked man was dripping blood down his left arm to the ground, but he used his right arm and threw a dagger into Lawrence's back. Lawrence staggered forward and then fell to the ground, dead. I turned back around and ran as fast as I could to get away from the cloaked man. I didn't know who he was or why he suddenly decided to kill Lawrence, but I couldn't stay around to find out if he wanted me dead or alive.

I had to slow due to my wounds and the cloaked man appeared in front of me. I stepped up to him and grabbed his money pouch. He stayed perfectly still and watched as I opened it and pulled out my bracelet. "This is mine," I said with as much steel in my voice as I could.

"I know," said Favian's voice.

I looked around, searching for him and then the cloaked man took off his hood and I stared in utter disbelief at the face of my best friend. "You? You're the cloaked man?"

He started to put the cloak around me, but I shied away from him. He frowned at me. "Marin, I had to play the part so I could find out where they were bringing you. If I hadn't gone along with their plan, I wouldn't have known where to find you."

"You left me down in that dungeon for four days!" I screamed at him. "I haven't had any food or water and I was almost raped and murdered!"

"Put on the cloak," Favian said. I was still pissed at him, but I took it and put it on, wrapping it around my body to cover myself. Favian said, "It's still the first day. I only pretended to leave the castle so he wouldn't expect me to come back and save you. That medallion only knocks you out for an hour at a time."

"Why did you take the bracelet?"

"I didn't want one of the other Mercenaries to take it. I took it for safe keeping."

Tears streamed down my face and I asked, "Why didn't you just kill them?"

"I'm sorry," he whispered as he grabbed me in a hug. "I am so sorry he hurt you. I couldn't kill the three of them. If I could have, I would have, I swear it. I am so sorry I failed you and allowed you to get hurt."

I pulled back from him, locking the emotions down to get back to what mattered. I saw blood on his arm and frowned. "You're injured."

He shrugged. "I have medicine in my saddle bags. You are the worst of us. We need to get you to a healer right away."

He put his arm around my waist and we walked slowly down the road. "You weren't supposed to come. You were supposed to stay back at the Academy and regroup," I whispered.

"If I had done that I never would have found you. This castle is hidden very well and is over fifty miles from home."

"How did we travel that far if I was only knocked out for one hour each time the medallion was pressed on me? I don't remember fainting that much."

"They used it on you as soon as you started to stir so you wouldn't even have been conscious yet," he said. He stopped and whistled loudly, calling for the horses. "I wanted to slit their throats every night, but the one with the scar was the only one who knew the way and he refused to tell us. I had to keep quiet."

"Why did you tackle me that day I tried to get away?" I asked softly.

"They were ready to kill you then. I had to neutralize the situation and tackling you and knocking you out was the only way to keep you alive."

Fire and Ice trotted up to us and Fire whinnied happily when she smelled me. I rubbed her nose and smiled. "Hey, girl." Favian released me, making sure I was leaning on Fire and then got his medicines and bandages from the saddle bags. "Let me help," I said as I sat down next to him on the road and helped him wrap the wound on his upper arm.

He sat still until I finished and then demanded to inspect me for injuries. I couldn't help the blush on my cheeks as I was forced to expose my naked body to him, but he was fast and it was over quickly. "You have bruises where he kicked and punched you, but nothing serious."

"I could have told you that," I said as I wrapped the cloak around myself again.

"I have extra clothes," he said as he reached inside

the saddle bags on Fire and handed me a set of clothes. "I figured yours would be dirty and you would want a change."

"How did you get both horses here? You weren't riding either of them."

"I had them following behind us in the forest where they wouldn't be seen."

"When did you train them to be able to do that?" I asked in shock.

He shrugged. "A little while ago."

He turned around and I quickly changed into my clothes, grunting with the movements, but happy not to be naked anymore. "Done."

Favian turned around and said, "We should get mounted and start home. I'm sure you want to get back as soon as possible." I nodded and tried to mount Fire, but was in too much pain. Favian pulled me backwards gently and tapped the center of the saddle. "Fire, lower please."

Fire dropped her front legs and then her back until she was lying down on the ground. "I didn't know she could do that either," I said in shock.

"I taught her that last spring when you hurt your back, but you were too stubborn to let me show you."

I climbed onto her back and clucked. She stood up and started walking. Favian mounted Ice and we headed South at an incredibly slow walk. Unfortunately, that was the fastest I could go with bruised ribs and even at a slow walk my ribs hurt with every step. We rode until the sun set and then made camp in the woods a mile from the road. I didn't have my sleeping bag so I was forced to share Favian's, but with the last few days I'd had, I was more than happy to.

He wrapped his arms around me, being sure to avoid my bruised parts and sang an Elvish lullaby to me, one which Mother used to sing to us. I sighed deeply when he finished and whispered, "Thank you."

"For singing?"

"For coming for me."

"I told you I would."

I rolled over and stared into his eyes. "I know, but it was incredibly dangerous for you to play one of them. If they'd seen your face, they would have immediately known who you were. You put your life in danger and I have no way to repay you."

He smoothed back my hair and said, "You being alive is payment enough."

The tears I'd repressed the days before all escaped and Favian held me as I cried. "I'm sorry I threatened you," I said once I was done crying.

Favian laughed. "That was a very impressive threat. If I hadn't known you couldn't get out of the binds, I would have been worried you would have killed me before you knew who I was."

I touched the sapphire bracelet and then settled against him. "Father must be furious right now."

Favian laughed. "Mother is probably threatening Macon and tearing apart the countryside in search of us."

"Macon didn't know you came after me?"

He shook his head. "No, they saw me get stabbed and then I disappeared into the crowd."

"Did you really get stabbed?" I asked him. He

lifted his shirt and I cringed at the hastily sewn wound. "You need to get that looked at."

"I know. There's a town half a day from here. I'll go to the healer in that town. Now, go to sleep."

I closed my eyes and relaxed against him as he started singing softly again. Just before I fell asleep, I heard him whisper, "I'm never letting you out of my sight again."

I would have argued, but it was the best thing he'd said all day. The trip home seemed to take a month, but that was probably because it had felt like the time was shorter since I was knocked out a lot. We found the town and ate until I felt like I was going to pop and then stayed in a room with a large soft bed. We passed all of the unfamiliar trails and I vowed to travel this way again so that I would become familiar with it and know how to get home should it happen again.

When we finally made it to the Academy, we found the doors open and chaos inside. Everyone stopped moving as soon as they saw Favian and me ride in.

"Is that…?"

"Look at her face."

"Did he…?"

Gossip began immediately and I really wished my face wasn't so black and blue and beat up looking. Macon ran from his office to us and asked, "Where the hell have you been?"

"Kidnapped, almost raped and almost murdered. Then saved by Favian and a long trip back here," I answered.

"I need you in my office now and I want a full

detailed report," Macon said.

I tried to dismount, but my ribs were still sore. I patted my saddle horn and said, "Fire, lower please." Fire laid down and Favian helped me out of the saddle.

"What happened to you?" Micah asked.

"I got punched in the face a few times and kicked in the ribs," I replied. "I feel great though."

"I'm glad to see you're alive."

"Someone send word to the Elves for me," Favian asked as he pushed me through the crowd that had gathered.

"Three cheers for Favian and Marin!" Master Martin yelled.

Everyone in the Academy yelled. "Hip hip hooray! Hip hip hooray! Hip hip hooray!"

I smiled as best as I could with my hurting face and Favian and I walked inside Macon's office. He immediately inspected me over and then Favian as well. "I have been worried out of my mind. What the hell happened? Why didn't you use your call? And where the hell did you go Favian?"

"It all started with a medallion," I began.

Two hours later we had covered every second of my journey with my black out moments filled in by Favian. I left out the parts of the conversation where Lawrence had tried to convince me that I wasn't human. For some reason, I didn't think Macon needed to know that. Favian told him the medallion was spelled to hurt whoever touched it and that it had been lost during the fight, but we both knew that wasn't exactly true.

Macon sat in silence for a few moments as he

absorbed everything that we'd told him. "Well, you've surely been tested to your limit," he commented. "I only wish things had gone according to plan."

"Nothing ever goes according to plan," I said cheerfully. "You should go get checked out by the healer."

"I'm fine," I started to say, but Macon gave me the look and I stood up. "Yes, Sir."

Favian and I headed slowly towards the healer's quarters and I tried my best to ignore the stares of the other students. "Why are you embarrassed?" Favian asked me as we walked.

"I just don't like all the attention, especially when you're the one who saved me. I would have died if I had been alone. Now everything must think I'm pathetic."

"They do not think you're pathetic. On the contrary, they think you're incredible," he said. "Not everyone could face their kidnapper and survive to get out."

I gestured to my face. "I didn't survive very well."

"You just need more practice," he said.

He stopped me just outside the healer's door and turned me to face him. "I think you're incredible Marin. You endured a lot and fought as hard as you could. I'm proud of you," he said with a strange smile.

"Now I'm even more embarrassed," I muttered as I walked into the healer's door.

"Marin!" the healer said happily. "I'm so glad to see you alive. Sit on the table."

I sat down and he began examining me. "Well, you seem to be healing well, but you really need a few days of bed rest."

"Yes, sir."

He stared at me in shock. "You're agreeing to bed rest?"

"For the first time, I don't have anywhere I have to be or any training that needs to be done. I am looking forward to bed rest."

He clutched his heart. "Oh dear, I think I'm going to have a heart attack."

Favian patted his shoulder. "She learned a little about herself on this adventure. I think she's actually turning into an adult."

"Oh no! An adult? How awful!" the healer teased.

I laughed and then groaned in pain. "Okay, no laughing."

The healer mixed up a tea of herbs and medicines and forced me to drink the disgusting drink. "This will help with your internal issues and will ease your pain. Now, go on and…"

"We're being attacked!" Micah yelled as he burst inside. "By who?" Favian asked as he drew his sword.

"Ogres," Micah said. "Hundreds of them."

I jumped down from the table and patted the healer. "Looks like bed rest will have to wait."

"There's the Marin I know," he said with a wide smile. "Go kick some ogre butt."

"You are in no shape to fight," Favian argued.

I pointed to the healer. "He just told me to go fight."

"Only because he knows you won't listen."

"So then why are you arguing?" I asked as I pushed open the door and ran outside.

The archers were lined up along the top of the gate and firing arrows as quickly as they could. I felt excitement and reached down for the power that lived within me. "Please, god and goddess assist me in killing these ogres."

"Your wish was fulfilled at your birth." A male voice said inside my head.

"Oh no," I whispered. "Now I'm going crazy."

"What?" Favian asked.

I shook my head. "Nothing, um, let's go." I charged forward and ran right passed Macon and the Masters and out the gate.

"Marin! You're going to get killed!" Master Sean yelled. Favian ran out with me and yelled back, "Just watch."

I took a deep breath and faced the ogres who had all stopped and turned to stare at me. "You are trespassing and attacking a school. If you do not turn around and leave this instant, I will be forced to kill you all."

"Leave some for me, okay?" Favian asked. I smiled. "Just try and keep up."

The strange fire filled me and I felt like a new person. An ogre charged at me and I ducked his fist and punched him in the stomach. He grunted and then growled angrily. Favian had kept hold of my swords and belt while I was kidnapped so I had them on now. I pulled my sword from my sheath and smiled. "I love my job." I sliced the ogre's left arm off and then sliced open his belly.

The remaining ogres bellowed in rage and I ran into the swarm of them, slicing, dicing and decapitating ogres around me. My blood churned with energy and excitement as I killed again and again. I could see Favian near me having as much fun as I was, but killing a third as fast as me. Was Lawrence right? Was I something other than human?

I didn't have time to think about it as the three hundred ogres continued to advance towards me. I killed and killed and killed and the wounds I had never bothered me. I felt so good and it felt so right to be killing these ogres. After an hour, the ogres were all finally dead and I was able to stop and relax a moment and observe my carnage.

Ogre bodies and pieces of ogre littered the field in front of the gate. It was incredible and I almost didn't believe that I was the one that had done it. Favian walked towards me and I took a step back from him. "I think he was right," I whispered. "I think Lawrence was right."

I had told Favian every word of my conversation with Lawrence so he knew exactly what I was talking about. "He only said that stuff to you to get you riled up. Come on, let's get inside."

"I can feel it inside me. I can feel this other part, this incredibly strong and fierce side just waiting to get freed. Killing these ogres opened it."

"You're talking gibberish now," he said softly as he moved closer to me.

"I need to figure out my destiny. I need to find out why I'm here," I whispered.

He grabbed my arms softly and said, "We will figure it out together. Okay?" I nodded and he wrapped his arms around me. "Let's go inside."

"Favian," I whispered. "Yes?"

"I'm going to faint again."

He caught me as I started to fall and then the world went black.

Falling unconscious was extremely irritating. I had fainted more times in the past month than I ever wanted to again in my life.

"Food," I muttered as I woke up and opened my eyes.

Favian leaned over me and said, "It's about time you woke up sleepyhead." He was trying to be teasing, but I could hear the concern in his voice.

"How long have I been asleep?" I asked as I sat up. "Three days."

I looked around and realized I was in my dorm and a second bed had been brought in and was right next to mine. "Have you been sleeping in here?" I asked in shock.

"Of course. I couldn't let you wake up alone," he said as he mixed something in a cup and then handed it to me. "Mother said to have you drink this as soon as you woke up."

I took the cup and gulped it down. "Are they

here?" I asked.

He nodded. "They're in the food hall right now. It's breakfast time."

"Where's the medallion?" I asked him.

"I gave it to Father who promised to have it locked up in our most secure area so that none will ever be able to use it against you again."

I sighed in relief. At least that was one thing I didn't need to worry about anymore. My stomach growled loudly and I rubbed it softly. "I need food."

He stood up and held out his hand to help me up. I started to get up and then I met his eyes. "I remember killing the ogres," I told him. "I also remember hearing a man's voice before the fight."

He sat back down and asked, "What did he say?"

"I had asked the god and goddess to assist me in killing the ogres and a man's voice said, 'your wish was fulfilled at your birth'. What the hell does that mean?"

He frowned in concentration and then shrugged. "I'm not sure, but let's keep the fact that you heard a voice in your head quiet for now."

I laughed. "Right."

He stood back up and held out his hand again. "Let's go eat."

I took his hand and let him pull me up, but then kept hold of his hand and forced him to meet my eyes. "Was I frightening?" I asked.

He gave me his serious face since he knew I was being serious and met my gaze with his own. "No, you were graceful and magnificent."

I was shocked by his answer and didn't know

what to say, but was saved when the door to my dorm opened and Father stepped inside. "Marin!" he said with a wide smile. "I am so glad that you're awake! You had us worried sick."

I stepped away from Favian and let Father envelope me in a warm hug. "I'm sorry I worried you," I whispered.

"Do not apologize, Daughter."

I pulled back and asked, "Father, what do you remember about when you found me?"

He sat down and sighed. "I had hoped to avoid this subject for a long time and especially not right after you regained consciousness."

"Please, I must know."

"When we found you, your family was dead, killed by the ogres and yet there were five ogre bodies lying dead on the ground beside your family. Kato and I watched in shock as a little, four-year-old girl used axes much too big for her to kill the remaining ogre and then sat down and wept. You were four years old and you had killed at least one ogre, but most likely more than that. It was impossible and yet we had witnessed it. After the ogre was dead you dropped the axes and started crying for your mother and father. I dismounted and walked towards you and you ran to me, wrapping your arms around my legs and asked for help. I fell in love with you immediately and picked you up and held you the entire ride back to the Elven Kingdom. And ever since, I have raised you as my own daughter."

"How could I kill an ogre at four years old?" I asked.

"Humans do things every day that are seemingly impossible," he said, but I could see he was hiding something.

"Did you ever regret taking me in?" I asked him.

He hugged me again and kissed the top of my head. "Never. Not even when you stole my horse or broke the one-thousand-year-old vase." He tilted my chin up and met my eyes. "How are you feeling?"

"I feel great, but I am starving and very confused and nervous," I answered him honestly.

He released me and said, "Well, then you two should be on your way. I'm off to talk with Macon."

I kissed his cheek and walked out of my dorm feeling slightly better now that I knew the truth of how he had found me. However, it raised even more questions than it answered. I had to be something other than human to have killed an ogre so young or wielded axes, didn't I?

Favian whispered something to Father and then caught up to me as we walked to the food hall. Favian opened the door and as soon as I stepped inside the mood in the hall shifted. Some looked at me fearfully and then most of the hall stood up and started clapping.

Master Martin walked up to me and patted me on the back. "Well done."

"Why, if it isn't the Little Death Bringer herself," Master Sean said.

Master Martin tapped his chin a moment and then smiled. "That's a perfect name for her. Everyone please show your appreciation to the Little Death Bringer for saving us from the ogres!"

"Woo! Death Bringer!" The group began cheering.

I walked by them all and up to the food line. The chef handed me a plate piled high with meat and bread. "I figured you'd be really hungry after using that much energy and sleeping for so long."

"Thank you," I said seriously.

"Thank you," he said. "You saved us all."

"I'm sure the others could have defeated the ogres," I mumbled, feeling somewhat embarrassed by all of the attention.

"Yes, but there would have been many injured and possibly some killed," he said as I walked away.

I walked to our table and sat down beside Mother who leaned over and kissed my cheek. "You look much better without the bruises."

"Thank you." I started eating and Favian sat down across from me, giving me a smirk, which meant he wanted to get in trouble by doing something we weren't supposed to do soon. That made me smile since it had been a long time since we'd gotten in trouble for doing something fun. Macon sat down at the table and I asked him, "So, did I pass the final test?"

He smiled. "With flying colors." He looked at Favian. "You didn't tell her?"

"I was going to wait until after we finished eating," he said. "Tell me what?" I asked.

"The graduation ceremony is in two hours," Macon said.

I gaped at him in shock. "Two hours?!"

"Where is she?" a familiar voice asked from the door of the food hall. I looked up to see Father's guard looking around with a bit of a frantic light in his eyes.

Kato finally spotted me and ran to me. He didn't say a word until he had inspected me over thoroughly. "You aren't injured anymore?" he asked. I shook my head. He slapped the back of my head with enough force to move it forward and then glared at me. "Don't you ever scare me like that again. I thought you were dead!" he said angrily.

I stood up and wrapped my arms around the Elf. "I missed you too, you old badger."

Kato hugged me back and then pet my hair like he used to do when I was a toddler and was frightened. "Little girl, you are so much trouble."

"And you love every second of it," I said as I pulled back to smile at him.

He smiled and said, "So, I heard you have a nickname now."

"Yes," Mother said angrily. "Though it is hardly fitting of a lady."

"Which is why it is very fitting for me," I said with a wink in her direction.

She sighed. "I tried so hard to make you a proper lady. You are just too stubborn."

"I can be a proper lady," I told her defensively. "When necessary."

"Really?" she asked unbelievingly. "Show me now then."

I stepped back from Kato and curtsied with my hands out like I was holding a dress. "I am honored by your visit, Kato. Would you like to join us for a cup of water?"

Kato bowed. "I would be honored, Lady Marin."

I walked to the water pitcher up by the chef and

holding the pitcher as if it were a porcelain tea pot, filled a cup of water. Once filled, I brought it back to Kato and sat it down in front of and then I sat down on the bench beside Mother. I picked up a piece of meat and chewed on it slowly with my lips perfectly closed, like a lady would. "My compliments to the chef! This is exquisite," I called out. "Now you're creeping me out," Macon said with a smile, but I could hear a bit of sincerity in his tone.

"Why sir! I am a lady after all!" I exclaimed and then nudged Mother who laughed loudly.

"Alright you've proven your point," she said. "Eat your food. I'm going to excuse myself so I don't have to witness your barbaric transformation."

I waited until she left and then plunged into my food. "This is so good!" I said happily around my mouthful of food.

The talking resumed in the hall and I was able to eat in silence. Favian waited until I was done and then tilted his head towards the door to indicate that he wanted me to follow him out. "Who sent the ogres after us?" I asked before standing up.

"That was supposed to be a failsafe for Lawrence. He told us that if he were to die, they would come. I thought it was a bluff," Favian said with a shrug.

"Well, it was a good thing we had Marin here," Macon said. "You were superb."

"Thank you," I said a little in shock since I had never received such high praise from Macon before.

Favian stood up. "We should go get ready."

I stood up and followed him outside. He pulled me in the opposite direction of the dorms and led me around to the stables, which were completely empty. He opened Fire's door and pushed me inside before bolting it closed behind us.

"What?" I asked feeling nervous. "Why are we hiding? What are we going to do? Paint something? Run away?"

He lunged forward and wrapped me in a tight hug, pressing his face against my head. "Stop trying to die on me," he whispered.

I stiffened in shock, having thought that we were going on some bit of fun and finding myself having to console him instead. I hugged him back after a moment and then patted his back. "I wasn't dead, just sleeping."

"Yes, but you were asleep for three days. We were worried you wouldn't wake up," he said as he continued to hug me. He pulled back and met my eyes. "I almost lost it when I saw him choking you," he whispered. "I wanted to gut him and torture him for days until he begged me to kill him."

I smiled and kissed his cheek. "That is the sweetest thing any male has ever said to me."

He stared at me a moment and then burst into a fit of laughter. He hugged me again and sighed. "You are my best friend and I refuse to allow you to get injured again. From now on, I am never leaving your side."

"You can't be beside me when I relieve myself," I said jokingly, though the thought of him standing beside me while I had to pee was a bit frightening.

"Obviously I'm not going to go that overboard," he said. "But I can't see you hurt like that again."

"Well, then I'll just have to be more careful."

"I'm serious, Marin. From now on we are going to act like real partners and stay by each other at all times. No more going off and playing the heroine. I will protect your life with mine if need be."

"Favian," I whispered. "You know I won't let you die for me."

He smiled and whispered, "You'll just have to try and stop me." He stared into my eyes a moment and then kissed me on the lips. His lips were warm and soft against mine and he tasted sweet. My body tingled in happiness and I felt like I was floating on a cloud. I had wanted this, even dreamed of it, and now it was happening. He pulled back, kissed my cheek and said, "I'm going to go get ready. You should as well."

I watched him go with the taste of him still on my lips and confusing feelings heavy within me. What had that been about? I felt giddy and nervous all at the same time. I sat down against the back of Fire's stall and closed my eyes. I knew now what the feelings I had been experiencing recently were.

I was in love with Favian. I loved my best friend. How could I have not figured out my feelings sooner? And how could I have allowed it to happen?

I knew I loved him and I also knew it was pointless. Despite the kiss he'd given me, he was the Elven Prince and I was just a human girl. I was ninety percent sure that he did not love me and I had to believe that or I would become bitter and overly jealous when he chose an Elven mate. I did not need the little bit of hope that that kiss had given me.

I clenched my fists and nodded. I would stay his best friend and partner and I would have to dismiss my love for him, pretend it didn't exist. As much as it hurt and as much as it was going to pain me, I had to do it for us. If I didn't, we wouldn't be able to work as partners and I refused to let that happen. It stunk that I had just discerned my feelings only to be forced to ignore them, but life was never fair.

I took a deep breath of Fire's familiar scent and the scents of the horses and hay around me to steady myself and then stood up. Fire nickered to me, so I patted her side as I walked out of her stall. I walked to my dorm, ignoring all of those around me to change and begin this new chapter of my life. Favian was right, I was growing up. I was turning into an adult and a woman. I also had a kick ass nickname!

Mother helped me change and insisted I at least put my hair up in a pretty ponytail. I knew better than to argue with the Queen and let her have fun putting my hair up and even let her put a little makeup on my eyes and cheeks to hide the slight bruising still there.

I headed to the outdoor training arena and took my place beside Favian in line for the ceremony to being. Favian looked at me and smiled. "Mother insisted, I take it?"

I smiled back. "Yes."

"It looks nice."

"Thank you," I said and ignored the butterflies in my stomach as I recalled our kiss.

Hundreds had gathered around the arena for the ceremony and I kept my smile in place. I was finally graduating. I was the first female to finish the Academy and I had earned my place. Part of me worried that Lawrence had been right about having Favian beside me, but I also knew that it didn't matter since he would always be beside me.

Macon stood on the stage that had been constructed in the center of the ring and raised his hands to get everyone's attention. "We are gathered here today to usher in a new group of Mercenaries and guards." He started the procession and one by one people went up and had their arm branded. I stood patiently waiting, but I began to worry when I was the very last student left.

Macon turned towards me and I could barely see him from the corner of my eye. "This was an incredibly challenging year and none had their values and talents tested more than our first female attendee and our first every female graduate, Marin," he said and clapped. The crowd clapped with him and I stepped out of line and walked up the stage to stand by Macon. "You have proven without a doubt that you are as skilled as the men and I am pleased to graduate you from this Academy and usher you into the life as a Mercenary." He pushed up my sleeve and the blacksmith pressed a hot brand into my arm.

I kept my face completely neutral and held in any visible signs of pain as they branded me. I would appear as stoic as the boys had and I would not give anyone a chance to belittle me.

"You not only passed all of our tests, but you also killed two hundred and eighty ogres on your own yesterday. You are a true example of a Mercenary and I know you will make this Academy proud, Little Death Bringer."

I smiled and then bowed. "Thank you, Sir."

I walked down off of the stage and every student in the Academy and every person attending started clapping a cheering. My infuriating female emotions started to take over, but I held the happy tears in and walked to Father who bandaged my arm and then cleared his throat. "We are all very proud of you and I believe now is the right time to give you these."

Kato stepped forward and held out two silver swords with ornate carvings on the pommels. "These were your father's swords," Kato said as he handed them to me.

"My father's?" I asked in shock.

"Your real father's," Father answered. "The one whom you must find."

"What?" I asked in shock. "What are you saying?"

"The humans that raised you were your family, the woman was indeed your mother who gave birth to you, but your true father was not the man who was killed by the ogres. You must find your father," Father said.

I looked at Favian. "Did you know?"

He shook his head. "I'm as shocked as you right now."

"How do I find him?" I asked.

"You will find clues along the way, but it will be a long road and dangerous."

Favian smiled. "That's no problem since she already has a partner."

"Why all the secrecy? Why didn't you tell me sooner?" I asked.

"We couldn't tell you sooner," Father answered. "We wanted to, but we were forced to swear an oath that we wouldn't reveal it until you started unlocking your powers. I want to tell you more, but your father has forbidden us from divulging anything else. He wants to see if you can find him."

"Why can't he just reveal himself?" I asked angrily. "It seems like a lot to do for a little reward." What did I care about a man that had never shown his face to me?

"Once you find him, he will unlock your true powers and give you one gift. To be given such things is a great honor and only those very deserving will receive them. Some never discover who he is."

"How many other kids are there?" I asked in shock.

"You are the first in quite a while," Kato answered. "There are none currently alive, as far as we know."

I took the swords because Kato was still holding them out and was shocked at how light they were. I spun them around a few times and then attacked an invisible villain. "Thank you," I said to Kato and Father.

"We also have a new belt for you since yours only has one sheath and isn't made properly for carrying two swords," Father said as he unwrapped a belt made by the finest Elven workers.

"It's beautiful," I said as I eyed the designs.

"Why does she get all the gifts?" Favian teased.

"Your gift is that you are relieved from Princely duties for the next three months so that you two can go start your conquests," Mother said. "But in three months you must return."

I hugged Kato, Father, and then Mother. "Thank you for everything."

"Go, Daughter of the Elves, and protect the country with your sword," Father said with a smile.

I put my new belt and swords on and then slipped the daggers Favian had given me into the slots in the belt.

"Marin and Favian, I have a job for you," Macon said as he walked towards us.

"Already?" I asked in shock.

He smiled. "It's a perfect job for you. There's a town about fifty miles south of here that has a dark forest bordering it. Inside there are three ogres who are reportedly kidnapping and eating people."

"I told you ogres are evil," I said to Favian.

He rolled his eyes. "So, our task is to find the ogres and kill them?"

Macon nodded. "Yes, and do it quickly."

I turned and smiled at Favian. "Ready?"

Favian smiled back. "I've been waiting on you."

I ran towards the stables and snatched up my tack, working on Fire as fast as I could. Favian was right beside me working on Ice, but I beat him to it and was mounted and riding out of the school with him trying to catch up. Life wasn't going to be easy and I still had lots of questions about my past and myself, but for now I was the happiest girl on the planet. I was a full-fledged Mercenary, my best friend was at my side, and we were off on our first official mission to kill the monsters I hated most in the world. Sure, I was in love with my best friend and I couldn't ever have his love in return, but we were partners and I had him by my side. And sure, I had learned that my father wasn't the human male I'd thought, but at this moment I had everything I wanted in life and I vowed to fight with every ounce of my strength to keep that the same in the coming years.

I am female and I am a Mercenary!

ABOUT THE AUTHOR

Catherine Banks is a USA Today bestselling fantasy author who writes in several fantasy subgenres and has multiple pseudonyms. She began writing fiction at only four years old and finished her first full-length novel at the age of fifteen. She is married to her soulmate and best friend, Avery, who she has two amazing children with. After her full-time job, she reads books, plays video games, and watches anime shows and movies with her family to relax. Although she has lived in Northern California her entire life, she dreams of traveling around the world. Catherine is also C.E.O. of Turbo Kitten Industries™, a company with many hats including being a book publisher and Etsy store full of nerdy fun.

Facebook: facebook.com/catherinebanksauthor
Twitter: twitter.com/catherineebanks
Amazon: amazon.com/author/catherinebanks
Bookbub: bookbub.com/authors/catherine-banks

MORE FROM CATHERINE BANKS

CHILDREN'S BOOKS
Calvin's Alien Adventure

**YOUNG ADULT PARANORMAL
& FANTASY ROMANCE SERIES**

Artemis Lupine Series
Song of the Moon
Kiss of a Star
Healed by the Fire
Battles of the Night
Artemis Lupine, The Complete Series

Pirate Princess Series
Pirate Princess
Princess Triumvirate

Little Death Bringer Duology
Mercenary
Protector
Little Death Bringer, The Official Coloring Book

**STANDALONE YOUNG ADULT PARANORMAL &
FANTASY ROMANCE BOOKS**
Monster Academy
Daughter of Lions
Lady Serra and the Draconian
Of Sky and Sea
The Last Werewolf
Sybil Deceived

ADULT PARANORMAL
& FANTASY ROMANCE SERIES

Zodiac Shifters Paranormal Romance Series
Centaur's Prize
Tiger Tears
Lion About

Ciara Steele Novella Series
True Faces
Barbaric Tendencies

ADULT REVERSE HAREM PARANORMAL &
FANTASY ROMANCE SERIES

Her Royal Harem Series
Royally Entangled
Royally Exposed
Royally Elected
Royally Enraged
Her Royal Harem, The Complete Series
The Demon's Fair
Her Royal Harem, The Coloring Book

Wings of Vengeance Series
Of Dragons and Cruelty
Of Minotaurs and Sacrifice
Wings of Vengeance, The Complete Series

Anderelle: Minloa Trilogy
Queen of the Stars
Empress of the Galaxy
Goddess of the Universe
Anderelle: Minloa, The Complete Series

Bonds of Madness Series
Sealing the Deal

Her Super Harem Series
Lucky Strike

Her Hellish Harem Series
A Demon's Heart
A Demon's Soul

STANDALONE ADULT PARANORMAL & FANTASY ROMANCE BOOKS
Demonic Contract
Dragon's Blood
Last Ama Princess
Transforming Rose
Alys of Asgard
Phoenix Possessed
Stone Heart

STANDALONE URBAN FANTASY BOOKS
The Pawn